THE SEVENTH'S
STAGHOUND

Books by Fairfax Downey

THE SEVENTH'S STAGHOUND
CAVALRY MOUNT
ARMY MULE
JEZEBEL THE JEEP
DOG OF WAR
WAR HORSE
INDIAN-FIGHTING ARMY

THE SEVENTH'S STAGHOUND

BY

FAIRFAX DOWNEY

ILLUSTRATED BY

PAUL BROWN

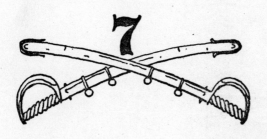

DODD, MEAD & COMPANY
NEW YORK   1948

PRINTED IN THE UNITED STATES OF AMERICA
BY THE VAIL-BALLOU PRESS, INC., BINGHAMTON, N. Y.

TO LAURA BRIGHT

As loyal and faithful to my family, over
many years, as Eliza to the Custers

CONTENTS

ILLUSTRATIONS

1: BIRTH OF A STAGHOUND

I

STANDING at rigid attention, the orderly saluted as much of the General as was visible. Since most of his Commanding Officer was underneath a side wall of his quarters, there was not a great deal to salute. But Army regulations require that an officer be saluted on recognition, and Private Fergus Mac-Tavish had duly identified the spurred boots and the seat of the blue breeches with broad stripes of cavalry yellow which now confronted him. Therefore his right hand snapped up to the brim of his campaign hat.

I

Regulations also direct that a salute be held until it is returned. There was no sign of acknowledgment except kicking legs, which seemed insufficient. Though it was a raw early morning in the cold winter of 1875, the orderly, stiff and straight, never even shivered. From beneath the house came the General's muffled voice, murmuring endearments, responded to by soft whines and whimperings. The keen blue eyes in Private MacTavish's dour Scot's face lit up and glowed.

Boots scuffled, and at last the officer emerged. His face was dirt-grimed, except for streaks licked clean by a canine tongue. Still he did not return the salute. He could not, for his arms were full.

"MacTavish," roared General Custer, "stop standing there like a statue! Give me a hand with these pups."

II

Before daybreak and the sounding of *First Call,* Eliza, the Negro cook, had called from the kitchen to the Custers' bedroom:

"Ginnel, that Maida she's gone. Cain't fin' that dawg nowhere."

Custer leaped up and flung on his uniform. He had known that Maida, the big Scottish staghound which was one of his favorites, would whelp soon and had been careful to call her into the house these cold nights. Now she had somehow broken out and, after the manner of her kind, gone off to have her litter in seclusion.

General Custer, some declared, often displayed more devotion to dogs than to people. Every horrible fate which might have overtaken Maida and her progeny raced through his head. Rattlesnakes usually stayed underground this cold weather, but some hungry reptile might have waked and crawled from its hole. Perhaps a pack of prowling coyotes had attacked, though they would never dare face a mother staghound unless crazed by starvation. Worst peril of all were the "friendly" Indians hanging around Fort Abraham Lincoln. An arrow through the throat would have finished Maida. Soon afterwards a kettle in some wigwam would have been boiling with a prized Indian delicacy—puppy stew!

But Custer's dash through and around the house had ended in his finding Maida and her litter safe beneath it. Nobody but the General or his orderly could have touched the big bitch with impunity; these two she loved. Now she walked proudly behind the master who was carrying her offspring. Beside her marched the Scot whom Custer some years ago had detailed and dubbed with a grin his Dog-Tender-in-Chief. No less proud than Maida, Scotty MacTavish let his hand rest on her noble head.

The splendid animal moved with the grace and dignity of her kind. Like the other staghounds in Custer's pack, Maida caught the interest of every newcomer to the 7th Cavalry, for her breed was little known in the United States. Scots first had brought staghounds to Canada. Among Maida's forebears perhaps was a mascot of one of the Highland regiments who often took these deerhounds or "rough greyhounds," as they sometimes were called, with them on foreign service. She belonged to the family of hounds of the chase, the group which includes Afghan hounds, Borzois or Russian wolfhounds, Irish wolfhounds, greyhounds, and whippets. Maida stood a good thirty inches high at the shoulders and weighed close to one hundred pounds—larger and stronger than the greyhound she resembled, and nearly as fleet. Her crisp, shaggy coat was red-fawn and her curved tail, carried like a banner, was slightly feathered, as were her legs. In full measure she was endowed with keen nose and eyes, speed, stamina, and courage—qualities in staghounds depended upon for centuries by the Highland clans to bring the antlered stag to bay—qualities which served General Custer as certainly when he hunted elk or the huge, humped buffalo.

Wild whoops from Custer heralded his entrance into the kitchen and on to the parlor with his armful of puppies, their mother, and the beaming MacTavish. The noise brought Mrs. Custer, hastening from the bedroom. As if by royal right, Maida lay down on the best rug and stretched out. The General knelt and with infinite gentleness placed his squirming burden at her side. Unerringly the still-unseeing puppies found their way to her dugs and resumed their interrupted breakfast.

A deep, admiring silence was broken by the cook Eliza. Since that day in the midst of the War Between the States when she had come into Custer's camp a slave, there to find freedom and give him and his a lifetime of loyal service, she had been a privileged character. Frowning down at the pups, Eliza began counting:

"One-two-three-fo'-five-six-seben! Lawsy, lawsy! Seben mo' dawgs crowdin' an' eatin' us outa house an' home!" Indignantly she demanded of Mrs. Custer, "Miss Libby, you know how many dawgs that makes we got? Fohty, Miss Libby! Fohty houn' dawgs!"

Lovely Elizabeth Custer smiled with resignation, knowing she could deny her beloved husband nothing. Anyway, a pack of only forty was an improvement. When they had been stationed in Louisiana and Texas after the War, the Custer kennels had been crammed and clamorous with no less than eighty.

"Ginnel, we got to get rid of these here." Eliza was unappeased.

"Seven new staghounds for the Seventh Cavalry!" Custer cried jubilantly. Then his voice grew reproachful. "Why,

Tavish, don't let me catch you neglecting my greyhounds or foxhounds," he said.

Suddenly Scotty stooped down again. "Alake!" he exclaimed sorrowfully. "The puir wee one!"

One of the pups, at first half concealed by two others of the litter, had been crowded out by them and lay revealed. He was weak and sickly-looking in contrast to his lusty brothers and sisters. Crawling feebly, he tried to find a dug again but could not until he was helped. Mrs. Custer uttered a little cry of pity, but the General remarked philosophically:

"Ah, well, we're lucky there's only one like that in the litter. He'll never run with the pack, that one. He can't live long. I hate to do it, but we'd best drown the poor little fellow. It'll give Maida a better chance to rear the rest."

Survival of the fittest—that was the law of nature. Here on the frontier its relentless working, for man or beast, was daily evident. The Indian Wars were just such a merciless test. Before the victorious white man, the red man was going down and though he was fighting his doom, it was sealed.

Tenderhearted Elizabeth Custer, tears in her eyes, opened her mouth to protest but shut it, words unspoken; her husband's will was law to her, and she knew what the decision had cost him as a dog-lover. MacTavish dared to plead. "Sir—" he began.

"That'll do," Custer shut him off. "Make it as quick and easy as possible, MacTavish."

Trustingly Maida let the orderly lift the puppy from her side. MacTavish could have carried the small creature in one hand, but he held him cradled in both arms as he strode out. For once he did not salute.

2: A TROOPER RE-ENLISTS

I

THE Army recruiting station at the Battery in New York City was enjoying a record day. An immigrant ship, which had docked the night before, started the ball rolling with a half-dozen German men and boys clumping into the station. Recruiting Sergeant Mike Quinn, seated at a table in the shabby front room, looked up, grinned broadly and rubbed his hands.

9

"Wie gehts! Wilkommen, Dutchies," he greeted them in German saturated with brogue. He had reason to be delighted. Germans often were the best recruits signed up by the U.S. Army these days, barring the Irish, of course. The big Bavarian leading this lot and two more plainly had already seen military service. They stood like ramrods, imitated by the others. It beat Sergeant Quinn how these square-heads fled conscription in the Fatherland and then had hardly stepped off the boat when they came running to enlist in our Army. Must be they needed a job. Perhaps the fact they now were acting of their own free will had something to do with it.

"Want to join up, do yez?" Quinn asked.

"Ja, mein Herr," the leader spoke up. *"Zu befehl."*

Quinn herded them in for examination by the surgeon.

The next applicants were not so promising. Came a furtive little man, who glanced nervously over his shoulder. Quinn's shrewd glance spotted him as a bank or store clerk. Likely they'd be finding a shortage in his accounts, and he was just a couple jumps ahead of the sheriff. Never mind. Sign him up—the Army needed recruits badly. Probably the sheriff would never chase him all the way out to the frontier.

After the clerk appeared a tall, thin fellow whose look of habitual meekness was half-submerged by an air of desperation. Quinn grinned broadly. Long experience had taught him types.

"And how did yez leave the Missus?" he inquired.

The thin man shuddered visibly. Undoubtedly running away from trouble at home. Rather than stand one more day of a shrewish, nagging wife, he was ready to face a whole tribe of yelling, bloodthirsty Indians.

"All right, all right," the sergeant said. "Pass the surgeon and you're in the Army." He bent a quizzical look on the fugitive husband and clerk. "Now the two of yez best give me a couple of nice new names. 'Should ould acquaintince be forgot?' " he sang, chuckling at his own wit.

Through the doorway floated the sound of raucous, drunken song, drowning the sergeant's voice. It was a hit from one of the Harrigan and Hart minstrel shows.

"There wush Shargeant John McCaffery and Captain Donahue.
Oh, they made us marsh and toe the mark in gallant Company 'Q'
Oh, th' drumsh'd roll. Upon my shoul, thish ish th' shtyle we'd go:
Forty milsh a day on beansh an' hay in the Regular Army, O!"

The singers, two Bowery bums, reeled in, supporting each other. Sign 'em up. The Army needed men even this badly. When they sobered up, they'd be sorry, but by then they'd be in uniform on a train bound for the West and it would be too late. That "forty miles a day" they were singing of so blithely would kill 'em or cure 'em. Quinn sighed. The Army had to take what it could get nowadays.

Now there was a turn for the better. To the grizzled man of soldierly bearing who stepped up to the table next, Sergeant Quinn spoke as one veteran to another.

"Want to re-up, soldier?"

"Sure do, Sarge."

"Previous service?"

"All four years of the War. Cavalry. Gregg's Division."

"Good outfit. Name and rank—hold on. Let's see yez walk across the room."

The veteran hesitated, then obeyed. He could not disguise a heavy limp.

"Sorry, soldier," Quinn refused him.

"Look here, Sarge," the man protested. "You sometimes take 'em with one arm and one eye. All I got is a game leg.

It's an old wound and it only troubles me once in a while. It's not infantry I want but cavalry. I can ride first-rate."

Quinn answered with gruff kindliness. "Like as not the surgeon'll pass yez. He was wounded, too, and he's got a wooden leg."

But it was the last recruit of the day that baffled Quinn completely.

The doorway framed a tall, sturdy young man. He stood erect, shoulders back. An eager light gleamed in his gray eyes. He took off his cap, revealing close-clipped, sandy hair. The sergeant could not help responding to the warmth of his engaging grin.

"And what can I do for yez?" Quinn inquired. This chap probably wanted street directions. Surprisingly the late-comer declared:

"I want to re-enlist."

"Do yez now?" Quinn spoke sarcastically. "It's one of thim college bys ye are and playing a prank. Be off."

"No, you're wrong, Sergeant. I have been to college at Yale for two years but I'm in earnest. I want to re-enlist."

" 'Re-enlist' is it? You're too young to join up for the first time."

"I'm not. I'm twenty-one."

"So? Name, former rank and rigimint?"

"Peter Shannon. Trumpeter, 'K' Troop, 4th Cavalry. Service in Texas in the Kiowa and Comanche campaigns in '73 and '74."

"Your papers." Peter produced them, and Quinn ran rapidly over them. One enlistment. Honorable discharge—character "Excellent." All in order.

Quinn grunted. " 'Tis a commission ye ixpect?"

Peter chuckled. "I never heard of those being passed out at a recruiting station. If I can win one from the ranks, that'd be fine."

"Gintleman ranker," Quinn sniffed. "Well, I'll ask yez no quistions—"

"And I'll tell you no lies."

"Go on in and see the surgeon and the officer and nivver blame Mike Quinn for what happens to ye."

For the second time Peter Shannon held up his right hand and took oath to serve his country in the Army of the United States.

II

Peter Shannon had been only a boy during the War Between the States, but even as a lad of nine he had served as a dispatch rider for the home guard of his native State of Pennsylvania, when it mobilized to meet the high tide of the Confederacy, flowing north to Gettysburg. In the years that followed, he and his father, a former captain of Union cavalry, had ridden together many miles, fighting over John Shannon's battles—a veteran re-living stirring skirmishes and valiant charges with his son.

Still vivid in Peter's mind were his pangs of regret that those gallant days were past and he had missed them. "You're lucky, Son," his father had assured him, "though it's hard for you to realize it now." And he told him of the many thousand brave men who had never returned, of the dreadful sufferings of the wounded, and all the grief, despair, and tragedy of war. "There's always a better way to settle arguments than fighting," John Shannon gravely insisted. "But men in their folly haven't learned that. Until they do, there are things worth fighting for. Freedom and the defense of the country you love. The way of life you believe is fair and honorable and true."

"But didn't the Southerners believe that, too?" Peter asked.

"I guess they did, Pete. Lots of them thought slavery was wrong. The Negroes could have been freed by peaceful means. But some Southerners put their States above the Union, and that was wrong. Well, it's over, and pray God we never see another war in my lifetime or yours."

But John Shannon was passing over the fact that the United States had begun fighting other wars when its great one was scarcely over—old wars flaring up again—the Indian wars. John Shannon more or less ignored them, like most of the country, but not the boys. Peter and his age were reading dime novels beginning: "The sharp crack of a rifle rang out, and another redskin bit the dust," and they were playing "Soldiers and Indians." In the West and Southwest blue-clad troopers were playing that game in grim earnest. Protecting the wagon-trains of the settlers and the railroad builders, they were fighting off the savage attacks of the red man, who was resisting the invasion of his hunting grounds to the death.

Incredibly Peter Shannon at sixteen had found himself plunged into the midst of it. On a summer visit to his uncle in Texas he barely escaped with his life from a bloody Kiowa raid in which his uncle and most of his wagoners were massacred. Enlisting in the 4th Cavalry as a trumpeter, the boy served through hard campaigns on the Staked Plains. In charges with drawn sabre he tasted the fierce joy of battle and learned that his father had told him truly of its bitterness when comrades were shot from their saddles and his best friend died under a Comanche lance. Yet a deep love of the Army had grown in him. It had been cruelly hard to obey when his family insisted, for the sake of his future, that he take his discharge and go to college.

Now—incredibly again—he was back in the Service once more, on a train steaming West to rejoin his regiment. It had happened so swiftly Peter had difficulty realizing it actually was fact. His mind ran through the last few months which had so altered his life.

The recent death of his beloved mother had left him in a state of such restless misery that he felt he could not endure to return to Yale and finish the spring term. He wanted to go back into the army, he told his father.

John Shannon shook his head. "If I'd known you were set on a military career, I'd have tried to get you an appointment to West Point when your time was up in the 4th Cavalry," he declared. "Otherwise there's no future. A commission from the ranks? You've got a Chinaman's chance, with the Army cut down to the size it is. Be sensible, Peter."

But in the end John Shannon gave in. Peter could buy his discharge next fall and finish college. In any event, his son was no longer a boy but a man. And in the heart of the former captain of cavalry a love of the Service lingered, too.

Back in the gallant 4th, on active duty in the Southwest! His mount, the black Morgan horse Justin, was with the regiment. So was his good friend and mentor, First Sergeant Sam Smith. So was the Adjutant, Major Lindsay—and so was the Major's daughter, Sally Ann. For two long years he had not seen them, although many letters, back and forth, had kept him in touch.

Of late months Sally Ann hadn't been writing very frequently. When he chided her in his letters, she explained that the post had been so gay with hops, picnics, and hunting parties that she'd been unable to find time to put pen to paper and, besides, she'd see him if she came East this summer. Usually when she did get around to writing, there was altogether too much mention of dashing young officers. Of course she had to have some fun, but such carryings-on were scarcely proper for an engaged girl. Hadn't she told him she'd wait for him always—that last night with the trumpets sounding

Taps in harmony when he held her in his arms and kissed her upturned lips?

Peter gazed out of the day-coach window at the big, yellow moon beaming down on the plains, as the train rattled through the night.

"Moon-struck, Shannon? What's her name?" The corporal in charge of the recruit detachment was standing in the aisle, grinning down at him.

"I was just thinking it'll be good to get back to the old outfit," Peter explained, reddening a little.

" 'Old' outfit? What do you mean 'old'?"

"What I say, Corp. We date straight back to the 1st Dragoons which became the 1st Cavalry. In '61 the first furnished *cadre* to form my regiment. It took part in seventy-six actions in the War. Since then it's seen a lot of tough Indian fighting. Yes siree, don't let anybody tell you different. It's a fine old outfit—the 4th Cavalry."

"The Fourth? Ha, ha, ha! You ain't going to the Fourth."

"The devil I'm not! I asked for my old outfit when I re-upped. That's my right as a previous service man. I asked the captain at the recruiting station."

"That old goat don't pay no attention to such stuff. I'm tellin' you this here draft and every batch of recruits that hits the depot at Leavenworth these days is marked for—"

"No! I'm going to the Fourth. I tell you—"

The Corporal guffawed loudly. "You're telling who, Soldier?" Mockingly he hummed the old bugle march: *You're in the Army Now.*

"Uh-huh, Private Shannon," he finished. "You're going to the 7th Cavalry, 'Old Curley'—Brevet Major Gen'ral, Lieutenant Colonel George Armstrong Custer, commanding."

3: CUSTER'S ORDERS

SICK CALL

I

SCOTTY MACTAVISH, the sickly staghound puppy in his arms, marched slowly away from Officers' Row. He headed across Fort Abraham Lincoln's broad parade ground, inclosed by quarters and barracks, toward the stables that lay beyond. There he would find a water bucket for the execution of his orders to drown the dog.

His steps began to drag until they slowed to the tempo of a funeral march. He groaned aloud and began to mutter over to himself lines from his favorite poet, Bobbie Burns— those moving stanzas to a little field mouse, its nest cleft open by a plowshare. Gazing down at the charge he carried, he recited:

> *"Wee, sleekit, cow'rin, tim'rous beastie,*
> *O, what a panic's in thy breastie!*
> *Thou need na start awa sae hasty,*
> *Wi' bickering brattle!*
> *I wad be laith to rin, an' chase thee,*
> *Wi' murd'ring pattle!"*

Destroying this puppy was bitter compulsion. Yet few soldiers dared disobey a direct order from Custer. Too well the Scot remembered that grim occasion in the South after the War when the General's brigade was doing unwelcome Reconstruction duty. One of his Michigan regiments had grown increasingly homesick. After being complimented on their smart appearance at a review, the men decided that it must be their soldierly qualities that were keeping them from discharge and home. The next day as sloppy and disorderly an aggregation as ever disgraced the uniform paraded. Here was mutiny or close to it, and Custer was furious. His blue eyes flashed fire and his yellow curls tossed like the mane of an angry lion. He put the whole regiment under arrest and commenced court-martial trials. One sergeant was condemned to death as the ringleader.

MacTavish, with a shudder, vividly recalled that day when the sentence was to be carried out. The entire brigade was drawn up under arms. Custer, though his life had been threatened, rode along the line, utterly fearless. A wagon rumbled up with the sergeant and a deserter seated on their coffins. The doomed men climbed down, were blindfolded and placed before a firing squad. "Ready!" and the carbines rose. Then, at the last moment, the provost marshal led aside the sergeant, granted a reprieve by Custer. When the volley rang out, the deserter died alone, but the sergeant keeled over in a faint. There was no further mutiny.

MacTavish, feeling queasy in his stomach, quickened his step. In the supply train's stables he laid the staghound puppy on a heap of straw, found a water bucket and filled it. His soul in torture, the Scot picked up the puppy again. Its warm little body snuggled against his broad chest. He pulled it away and poised it over the bucket.

II

No! He would not. But he must. Before this he had mercifully destroyed dogs dying of distemper or suffering from a fatal injury and he had done away with just such sickly puppies as this.

But never a staghound. That made the difference.

Man has always picked a favorite among the hundred or more breeds of dogs he has developed. An embracing fondness for all dogs he may have, but usually one variety stands first in his heart. So it was with this American soldier who as a young man had come over from Scotland where the staghound or Scottish deerhound was prized above all the canine kind. That native of the Highlands was all the more cherished because he nearly had become extinct in those desperate years after the Battle of Culloden, in 1746, when Bonnie Prince Charlie and the clans had met bloody and final defeat at the hands of the English. Had not Sir Walter Scott himself acclaimed the staghound, mighty in strength and stature, faithful and courageous, as "the most perfect creature of Heaven"? Could a Highlander drown a hound of that breed, however weak and sickly, when skilled care might save it?

Never! MacTavish drew back and thrust the pail aside with his foot.

He knew the risk he ran. Custer seemed to have a way of discovering almost everything that happened in the regiment.

The pup would have to be well hidden and milk provided for him.

Sudden inspiration struck the Scot. Yonder in his stall stood Old Pizen, the meanest mule in the 7th Cavalry's wagon-train. Nobody ventured into that stall except Old Pizen's driver and he entered it only with reluctance. Far better than an iron-studded door, under lock and key, were that mule's heels. His stall could serve as sanctuary for the staghound puppy. The driver, a friend of MacTavish's, would keep his mouth shut.

Scotty walked over. He spoke in the soothing tones of one who understands animals. Old Pizen's long ears swiveled around but did not lie flat back against his neck. He listened with attention, and the ears flipped appreciatively. Here plainly was a man aware of the dignity and sterling worth of a much-abused and put-upon mule. At Scotty's request, Old Pizen moved over, and the orderly entered the stall and made a bed for the pup in straw underneath the manger. The mule lowered his head to the length of his halter, emitting a gentle snort. Evidently the guest was welcome.

MacTavish's mouth set in a straight line of satisfaction. General Custer, who had charged Rebel batteries and Indian villages sputtering with the fire of repeating rifles, would not lightly face the terrific wallop packed by Old Pizen's hind-quarters and iron-shod hoofs.

III

For days the life of the staghound hung in the balance. Scotty lavished painstaking nursing on him and all his wisdom in the care of dogs. He spent his pay for milk and even dared borrow an occasional cupful from Eliza; she gave it with grudging suspicions but said nothing. Old Pizen stood vigilant guard over his ward. Despite Custer, Pizen's driver and the soldiers who saw the puppy kept mum, enjoying slipping something over on the Old Man.

At last it became unmistakable that the dog would pull through and do his part to carry on his ancient breed, dating from the early Sixteenth Century. The once feeble little animal waxed so active, MacTavish had to make a small harness for him and tie him to a staple in the stall or he would have wandered out through the stable. His coat, more yellow than sandy red like the rest of his litter, grew with richness. His body developed strength and sinew.

Dark brown eyes, black-rimmed, watched eagerly in the shadows of the stall for Scotty. Yips of joy, quickly hushed, greeted him.

"So you ken me," said MacTavish, petting him. "Then must you be known to me. It's time you bore a name."

MacTavish did not need to take long thought. His name must be Bran.

Famed in legend and tales of the Highlands and in life as well is the name of Bran, the Staghound. In Gaelic myth he was the dog of Fingal, hero of Caledonia—ancient Scotland. So fierce a guardian was that huge hound, his master must needs tie him when he engaged in a single combat with an enemy champion, and nothing less than a stone pillar served to hold him when he plunged against his chain. In after years every superior staghound was likened to Bran; a proverb ran, "If not Bran, it's Bran's brother," and that was the highest compliment Scots could pay. MacTavish in his own boyhood in Scotland had known a famous dog that bore the name. That Bran in 1844 had singlehanded killed two unwounded stags in forty-five minutes.

"Ay, you are well named, Bran," MacTavish told his dog.

Bran grew fast—puppy yips changed into deep-throated barks. MacTavish or the stable guard hushed him, and he fell obediently silent, but sooner or later he would betray him-

Old Pizen lowered his head to the length of his halter, emitting a gentle snort. Evidently the guest was welcome

self. He would have done so already except that Custer's dogs roamed everywhere around the post, and the young staghound's soundings-off were mistaken for theirs. Not much longer could he be kept tied up in Old Pizen's stall, with stealthy walks on leash at night, given him by Scotty, as his only exercise. His health demanded that he be loosed to go bounding across the plains in the runs and hunts that were his birthright.

In increasing distress poor MacTavish cudgeled his brains. What was he to do? Add Bran to the pack and trust he would never be noticed among so many? That would never do. General Custer knew every one of his dogs intimately and would be certain to spot the newcomer. If he did discover Bran's identity, then might he welcome the fine dog his orderly had succeeded in raising against all odds? Not Custer. He never forgave disobedience of orders.

Scotty sat in the dark stable with his arms around Bran's neck and mourned. His attachment to this creature whose life he had saved had grown close. Now his Scot's logic told him that two moves only were possible. He could ship the dog to his sister in Canada, or risk the action his commanding officer would take when he found the dog. The Scot knew well enough what that action would be. The animal would be sent away anyway, and Private Fergus MacTavish would find himself in the guardhouse.

"I canna part wi' thee," he whispered in broad Scot's into a silken ear. Bran wagged his tail violently and licked the hands around his neck. "But I maun. I maun send 'e awa, to be my dog nae mair."

Through the doorway he watched without interest a detachment of recruits arriving at the post. He could have no inkling that in their ranks marched the answer to his dilemma.

4: A QUESTION OF REGIMENTS

ADJUTANT'S CALL

I

A SERGEANT with a tongue that stung like the lash of a bull-whip marched the recruit detachment up the road to Fort Abraham Lincoln, paying particular attention to the rear of the column.

"Heads up, shoulders back, you bunch of baboons!" he barked. "Try and look like the soldiers you ain't. 'Twas a bad day for the Seventh when it drew a lot of rookies what march like they was in a sack race."

The sergeant's comparison was painfully apt, as sergeants'
remarks often are. Most of the recruits shuffling along in
new cavalry boots, their dark blue blouses hanging in folds
and their lighter blue breeches a size or so too large—
company tailors would have plenty of alterations to make—
did resemble animated sacks.

"Eyes front, you Bowery bums!" he roared. "Don't be
lookin' back at them saloons in Bismarck 'cross the river,
with your tongues hangin' out. It'll be many a day 'fore you
get a pass into town, or a snort at the sutler's, either. 'Fore
then I'll sweat that rotgut licker outa you!"

The absconding clerk still was glancing furtively about
him, but the runaway husband, basking in new-found freedom, had become jaunty and smiling.

"Wipe that silly smile off your mug, you!" shouted the
sergeant. "Think you don't gotta know how to march in the
cavalry? Think all you do is traipse around on the back of
some poor, long-sufferin' hoss, do you? I'll learn you. Get in
step, you." He started chanting cadence:

"Left, left, left, right, left. Left, left, left my wife and
forty-seven children."

The fugitive husband moaned, recoiled and stumbled into
the file ahead, while the sergeant roared sulphurously at
him and chanted again:

"Left, left, had a good home and he left."

A ripple of laughter ran through the ranks. The sergeant
yelled for silence and reminded his charges that they were
marching at attention. Plaintively, he besought anyone to
explain the affliction of such a draft on a deserving and re-
spectable regiment. Except for the first squad, he declared,
this was the most worthless and unutterably hopeless batch
of recruits it ever had been his misfortune to encounter in
twenty years of service.

Since General Custer and other officers likely would be

watching, the sergeant had formed his first squad craftily.
The big Bavarian, a foreign decoration on his chest, marched
as guide. Peter Shannon was Number One; a single stripe
or "hash-mark" sewn on his left sleeve showed he had
served one enlistment. Beside him Jim Galt, the veteran,
tried hard to disguise his limp; he wore two hash-marks
and a Corps badge. Germans completed the squad. Custer
would view the head of the column with approval—if he
did not notice the black scowl on the face of the Number One.
Peter was still boiling with furious resentment at the care-
less indifference or deliberate disregard of the recruiting
officer who had railroaded him into the 7th Cavalry in the
face of his request to rejoin his old regiment.

"Chirk up, young Shannon," Galt urged out of the side
of his mouth. "Don't go causing trouble for yourself."

Ever since hearing Peter's angry complaint, the veteran
had been arguing against his making an issue of it. "Wait
your time," he advised. "The Seventh's a pretty fair outfit.
It fought all right in a lively scrap with the Cheyennes at the
Washita and it has made some good scouts. There's real
action ahead, I hear tell. Trust Custer for that. My brigade
charged alongside his in the War, and he's a fighter, if there
ever was one. Don't be bullheaded now. You know the
Army. No C.O.'s going to transfer a previous service man
with a good record, not if he can help it. Keep quiet and write
your people in the Fourth to put in for you."

But Peter would not listen. Hardly had the recruit detachment entered the post when he was demanding an interview
with the Adjutant.

"All right, all right," growled the sergeant. "That's just
who you're seein'. Colonel Cooke's gotta assign this crow-
bait to the diffrunt companies and when most of 'em see what
they get, there won't be no long, rousin' cheers."

II

The formidable figure of the Adjutant loomed over the young soldier who entered the office, removed his cap and snapped to attention. Cooke stood close to six feet-four in his boots. A magnificent pair of those whiskers, christened "burnsides" or "sideburns" after the Union general, Ambrose Burnside, jutted out from his cheeks. Without make-up, he could have stepped on the stage and played the British character, "Lord Dundreary," in *Our American Cousin* or, donning helmet and cuirass, have ridden with the British Lifeguards, unsuspected as a Yankee. His fellow-officers of the Seventh called him "Queen's Own" Cooke. In the War he had won brevet rank—an award for gallantry or merit—of lieutenant colonel, but now, in the reduced Army, his actual rank was first lieutenant.

"Sir," Peter addressed him, "Private Shannon, recruit detachment, has permission to speak to the Adjutant."

"Wait till I look over your papers. Stand at ease." As he read, Cooke spoke half to himself. "*Mmmm*. Fair enough. One enlistment. Active service in Texas. Like to have been in that Palo Duro affair myself. Ah! A trumpeter. That'll tickle the General. We've got the best music in the Service. The band always plays the Seventh into action. You're in luck, Trumpeter."

Peter could no longer contain himself. A torrent of wrathful expostulation burst from him. He dressed down the recruiting officer in terms referred to in the Articles of War as "disrespectful and insubordinate language toward a superior officer." His loyal acclaim of the 4th Cavalry demoted every other regiment in the Army to the rank of a disciplinary battalion. He'd serve in the Fourth or nowhere, he ended defiantly.

Cooke heard him out, then said calmly: "Been a civilian

too long, haven't you? You'll have to learn again how a soldier talks—and how he obeys. Application for transfer denied. That's all."

His face crimson, Peter answered through set teeth: "I want to see the Commanding Officer. That's my right, according to regulations, and you can't deny it."

"Guardhouse lawyer, eh?" the Adjutant remarked. "All right. Go ahead and see General Custer, and Heaven help you!"

III

It was unfortunate that Peter found Custer on horseback. Any man on foot is at a disadvantage when he must look up at a mounted man, and when the rider was George Armstrong Custer, that heroic figure whose dashing war exploits and Indian fights were already an American legend, then the handicap was increased a hundredfold. But Peter was too angry to be awed. He spoke out vehemently.

Custer was forebearing. He liked the looks of this clean-cut young fellow. Despite his own fierce pride in the Seventh, he did not resent Peter's paeans to the Fourth.

"I understand," he said soothingly. "You're right, the 4th Cavalry is a first-rate regiment. I knew General Mackenzie, a fine leader. His Adjutant, Major Lindsay, is a friend of mine. That pretty little daughter of his—"

Peter, diverted for a moment by the mention of Sally Ann, flared up again and repeated his demand for transfer. Still unruffled, Custer replied:

"I'll consider your transfer later. Meanwhile, give the Seventh a chance, soldier. I've got a vacancy for a corporal-trumpeter, and you're in line for it."

"I don't care about any rank here, sir," Peter stormed. "All I want is my right to—"

Few dared face up so to Old Curley. The continued restraint of the quick Custer temper was remarkable.

"Listen," the General ordered evenly. "There's fighting ahead for the Seventh. Every sign points to a big campaign against the Sioux and Cheyennes before the summer's over. No soldier with your record would want to pull out on the eve of action."

Peter lost control. "I tell you," he shouted, "the Fourth has seen more action and will see more than the Seventh ever—"

He gasped, stricken into sudden silence. Never would he forget the apparition glaring down on him. Sparks seemed to shoot from the blue eyes. Clenched teeth shone white under the bristling moustache. Confederate troopers and red warriors had seen that look just before a flashing sabre cut them down.

General Custer yelled to an orderly standing some distance away.

"MacTavish, take this recruit to the captain of Headquarters Company and tell him the man's to have two weeks' stable police on my orders. If there's any further trouble, he's to stand a court-martial."

A shaken young soldier saluted, faced about and followed the orderly.

5: DOG AND MASTER

I

"GOVERNMENT ghosts" was Army slang for stable police because of the white garments they wore to protect their uniforms. Peter Shannon, clad in his stable frock, looked like a particularly forlorn and disconsolate wraith. Never before in his military career had he been given company punishment; it would stand against his record. And his chances of rejoining his beloved 4th Cavalry seemed more remote than ever.

As a severer penalty for his insubordinate conduct, he had been assigned to the mule stables of the supply train, a duty dreaded by many soldiers. Mules are far more jealous of their rights than the average horse—rights earned by hard labor. With heels or teeth they resent trifling, roughness, or indignity. Yet, once they sense you would treat them justly, you seldom have trouble with them. Peter, who had learned how to handle mules in the 4th Cavalry, had no difficulty.

Long ears failed to flaunt a danger signal when, speaking softly, he entered a stall.

He plied brush and shovel with vigor, taking no chance on a court-martial. Day after day of backbreaking work dragged on. If a man rode or drove an animal, caring for it was much less of a chore. But this business of being chambermaid for scores of other men's mules was no bed of roses. Peter, remembering from his mythology that Hercules had cleaned the Augean stables by turning a couple of rivers into them, often thought that he would be willing to dig a channel from the Missouri River through to the supply train stables for the same purpose.

But there was one stable he was spared—there was something mysterious about that. Why was he never sent to Stable B? His curiosity increased.

Then one day a new corporal in charge of the stable police detail ordered Peter down to B. "I'll give you a pointer, rookie," the non-com warned him. "Watch out for the big mule in right corner stall at the far end. His name is Old Pizen and he lives up to it. If those heels of his ever get a good swipe at you, you'll go out through the roof. They'll pick you up in Bismarck across the river and turn you in for being in town without a pass."

"Thanks, I'll watch out," Peter answered. "I've got troubles enough."

He worked down the stable toward Old Pizen. As he approached, he began to hear strange sounds. That was barking, not braying. Some dog must have strayed into the mule's stall. A noise of scuffling and snorts, punctuating the barks, indicated that the canine intruder was taking long chances on mayhem or sudden death. Peter dropped his implements and broke into a run, struggling out of his encumbering frock.

He saw a half-grown staghound standing on his hind legs in the stall and pawing at Old Pizen's ribs. Bran, broken loose from his tether under the manger, was playing with his long-eared friend. Pizen bent back a supple neck and nipped at him genially. The barks and snorts waxed louder.

"Here, here," Peter called. "Fun's fun but somebody might get hurt. You come out of there, pup. Here!" He whistled to the dog urgently.

Bran looked around but paid him no other heed. He did not know this soldier. His tongue lolled out in a canine grin and he barked joyously in his sport with Old Pizen. Now a strategic move occurred to him. He shifted back to the mule's haunches where nips could not reach him. Here he could do a bit of nipping of his own. In the manner of his forefathers pulling down a stag, Bran took hold of Old Pizen's right hind leg just above the hock.

Peter shouted frantically. "Let go! Come here, sir. You'll get kicked to Kingdom Come!"

Bran meant to take only a light grip. But he did not know his own young strength and the sharpness of his teeth. Old Pizen emitted a squeal of startled pain. He swung his big body to one side, crowding the dog against the side of the stall. More than a few times mules have crushed men to death with that maneuver. Bran gasped and loosed his hold. Half stunned, he dropped to the floor directly behind the mule. It took Old Pizen only a second to regain his balance. Then the mighty haunches flexed. Heels drew back for that terrific kick which no other creature can match. Only man's invention of gunpowder and some of his great machinery, such as triphammers and piledrivers, surpass it.

Peter yelled so loudly in alarm he could not hear the shouts of the newly-arrived MacTavish and the corporal from the doorway. He seized the bare second he had to act. A lightning dive and he had grabbed Bran's limp body and thrust it aside. Wildly he scrambled for safety.

Too late. Iron-shod heels hit him with a thud that brought

*Wildly he scrambled for safety. . . . Too late. Iron-
shod heels hit him with a thud*

groans of anguish from MacTavish and the corporal running
to the rescue. One hoof grazed his skull, the other drove into
his ribs. He was flung clear across the stable aisle. His whole
frame shuddered convulsively, then lay inert and still.

"The poor fool!" cried the corporal, bending over Peter
sadly. "What'd he want to go and get himself killed for—
just for a dog. Can't understand it."

"You wouldna," said MacTavish shortly. "Run for the
surgeon. Quick, mon!"

II

The secret of the hidden staghound no longer could be
kept. A full report of a possibly fatal accident to a soldier
must be made. A board of officers would sit and determine
whether Private Shannon's injuries or his death were incurred
in line of duty. A verdict to the contrary was virtually certain on the evidence to be given by the witnesses who had
seen most of the incident. No military necessity could have
caused the young trooper, lying in the post hospital still unconscious, to risk his life for a dog.

First of all, the presence of the dog would have to be explained—and that to General Custer even before the board
convened. MacTavish sat in the stable and wracked his
brains. Beside him crouched Bran, already recovered, for he
had been little hurt. A leash was fastened to his harness in
readiness. Custer, the Scot well knew, would be sending for
them both any minute.

Before MacTavish could work out his problem, the inevitable summons arrived.

The Dog-Tender-in-Chief found Custer just returned
from an early ride, on which the greater part of his pack had
accompanied him, as usual. Most of the dogs had dashed off
to their breakfasts, but one fat and aging foxhound named

Lucy Stone had taken position in front of him. She still was puffing; she seldom exerted herself anymore and on a march she generally asked for a lift in a wagon. Plainly she was regretting the run this morning, for as she sat in front of the General she lifted beseeching eyes to him and held up a forepaw to display a cactus thorn sticking in the pad. If no human were near, the dogs could pull out thorns with their teeth, but everyone of them knew they never asked Custer for help in vain.

Still in the saddle of a fine Kentucky thoroughbred, his favorite mount Vic, Custer looked down at the fat hound. As always with his dogs, he began talking to her, putting in her mouth the words she would have spoken if she had the gift of speech.

"There sits Lucy Stone," he declared. "And she is saying, 'If you please, sir, since you chose to bring me into a land of bristling earth like this, will you please get down immediately and attend to my foot?'"

He swung down and with a pair of tweezers in a knife he carried for the purpose gently extracted the thorn. Lucy wagged her tail and waddled off, Custer telling her she was welcome.

Then he turned toward the orderly and his charge. Long and hard he stared at Bran. His expression softened as he took in the points of the fine animal. He fondled the staghound, and Bran responded politely. Then he accused suspiciously: "MacTavish, I've seen this hound before."

"The General has seen the like of him," MacTavish evaded, "but nane better in a' his pack." The Scot took a bold step. "It may be, sir, the General marks some resemblance to the puir, sick pup I put out of the way." (Well, he *had* put him out of the way—in a way.) "Where's the likeness to this strong one? Maida's litter was sandy red. This one's yellow."

Custer, still more than a little sceptical, demanded:

"Whose dog is he?"

Scotty had been thinking fast and furiously. "Whose dog, sir? That I wouldna want to tell, but wi' the accident to the lad in the hospital, I can nae longer keep it." Mentally, he presented a surprise gift to Peter. "The dog is his—his very ane."

The General looked flabbergasted, then indignant. "Mean to say that young trumpeter who kicked up such a fuss about wanting to rejoin the 4th Cavalry dared sneak a dog into the post?"

None of the guile and craftiness with which the Scot now spoke showed in his face. "Who would hae said him nay in his auld regiment where he thought to go?" he asked. "Small wonder he's avairse to serving wi' the Seventh, feeling he must give up the fine young hound who has his heart."

Here was a serious flaw in MacTavish's plot and he knew it. There was no telling whether the young soldier in the hospital would agree to having a staghound suddenly foisted on him as his own—even if the animal were the one he had saved. And should he happen to be willing, would he be quick enough to play up to MacTavish's lead, if ownership had to be established in General Custer's presence? Well, those chances would have to be taken. Meanwhile, Scotty told himself, he must make every effort to get to the hospital, as soon as visitors were allowed, and prime Private Shannon.

While such apprehension flashed through his head, the Scot continued spinning his yarn for Custer.

"Ay, now the General canna mistake the lad's reason for wanting to leave the regiment. How could he ken that a staghound—in particular so bonnie a one as this—could nowhere find a warmer welcome than in the Seventh?"

Suspicion was replaced on Custer's face by a rare expression of indecision. MacTavish hammered in still more of the overwhelming posers which had his commanding officer backed into a corner.

"If Private Shannon lives, might the General not make him his ane trumpeter, to follow him on his rides and hunts?" the orderly resumed. "And then wouldna Bran here run wi' the General's hounds?"

"MacTavish, you're a scheming scoundrel!" Custer burst out, laughing.

"Nae, sir," Scotty answered, all innocence.

Custer said reflectively: "That young soldier must be devoted to his dog when he takes what he took from Old Pizen's heels for this pup's sake."

" 'Greater love hath nae mon,' sir," quoted the Scot solemnly.

III

Not for some days could the Surgeon feel assured that Peter Shannon would recover. Gradually the effects of the brain concussion sustained by the young trooper wore away, and broken bones began to knit. By a twist of his body as he snatched Bran aside, Peter had escaped the full force of the mule's kick; otherwise he would have paid a far more severe penalty than three cracked ribs and a gashed scalp.

Although there were few comforts in the hospital of a small frontier post, Peter was well aware that he was lucky to have been gravely injured in garrison and not in the field. Too often on campaigns no surgeon was present. A soldier, wounded or injured, could count on nothing more than crude first-aid from an officer or fellow-troopers. Many a time the best he could do was tear off a strip from his dirty shirt, bind up his wound and hope to obtain proper treatment before it turned gangrenous. Peter had seen occasions in the Fourth when badly wounded men were tied in their saddles to ride long, agonizing miles. A hard-jolting ambulance was a comparative luxury, one seldom enjoyed by fast-moving cavalry, who could not be delayed by wagons. No man, if it possibly could be avoided, ever was left to the mercies of the Indians while a spark of life remained in him.

Mrs. Custer and other Army women, along with the kindly Eliza, helped the none-too-capable hospital orderlies nurse Peter toward health. Chaplain O'Neill came often to sit with him. Praising Peter's brave rescue of the staghound, the chaplain drew on his lore of dogs to entertain the convalescent.

"It's usually the other way around, Shannon, with the dog saving a man," he observed. "There's St. Roch, for instance. He was a holy man who tended the sick in medieval times when the plague raged through Europe. One day he was himself stricken and lay alone and helpless in a forest. A dog found him and every day brought him a loaf of bread in its mouth. You can see St. Roch's image in many a European shrine still, with the faithful hound, the loaf in its mouth, crouched at his side. You'll also find dogs represented lying at the feet of other saints, especially St. Bernard."

"I've read of St. Bernard dogs," Peter said.

"Marvelous animals," the chaplain declared. "I saw something of them when I was a young man, studying abroad, and made a trip up to the Great St. Bernard pass in the Alps. The monks of the Hospice there began keeping those big dogs, descendants of the Molossian hounds of the Romans, back in the seventeenth century. You can imagine what fine company they were for the good brothers, lonely in their monastery in the snow-clad peaks. When the monks went out to search for travelers, lost in a blizzard, they took their canine friends along. Not only did the dogs help break paths through the drifts but their keen noses scented helpless people no man could have found. Soon the monks began sending out packs of three or four on patrols by themselves. When the St.

Bernards found a traveler lying in the snow, they would offer him a restorative from the small cask of brandy slung around their necks. Then two would crouch down beside him and warm him with their bodies, while another plunged back to the Hospice to give the alarm and bring rescuers, guiding them often through a blinding snowstorm. They say the number of human lives those dogs have saved runs into the thousands."

"I wonder how the dogs are trained," Peter interjected.

"The monks told me all they do is send out a young dog with older ones on a patrol," answered the chaplain. "The rest is instinct and the dog's abiding love of mankind."

"One of them was named Barry, I remember."

"Yes, he was the most celebrated of them all. The dogs were called 'Barry hounds' after him before they were known as St. Bernards. Barry alone rescued forty people. There's a legend that the forty-first person he tried to save killed him, mistaking him for a wolf, but the truth is he lived to a ripe old age and was painlessly put to sleep—about 1814, I think it was. I saw him, mounted by a taxidermist, in a museum in Berne, Switzerland.

"Now this staghound of yours, Shannon—"

"He's not mine, Padre. I never saw him before that day in the stable."

"Then he belongs to MacTavish, I suppose," Chaplain O'Neill guessed. "But since he's not yours, then far greater credit is due you for putting your life in jeopardy that day to save him, no more than a strange dog to you."

The Chaplain rose and stood beside Peter's cot. Smiling down at the prostrate young soldier, he said:

"I've told you that the account between man and his friend the dog is heavily in the dog's favor. You have helped to cancel some of that debt. God's blessing on you, my son."

IV

Custer's admiration had been aroused by Peter's coura-geous act in saving the dog. His fondness for dogs had been played upon with infinite skill by MacTavish. But the Gen-eral was too old a hand not to know the wiles of soldiers and to swallow their stories whole, however glibly told. He was not altogether satisfied. He would investigate further.

With Private Shannon now well enough to be questioned, Custer was ready to settle his doubts about the dog. He set off on a tour of the post, picking up MacTavish and Bran en route. Before the Scot realized that they were bound for the hospital, they had arrived. He had no time to set the stage, nor had he been allowed to see Peter previously and explain the situation.

As Peter lay in his cot, he felt a stir run through the ward. The regimental commander was paying a visit, and behind him marched his orderly leading a dog. Peter's gaze warmed. It was the dog he had rescued that day.

As if he were making a routine inspection, General Custer walked down the room, asking patients how they were getting on. He planned to reach Peter's bed last. Then he would see whether the dog greeted his "master"—or whether he even noticed him.

But the canny MacTavish had thought ahead to that one. It might well happen that Bran would not heed the soldier at all, or that the dog would overlook him if led casually past. Then the whole careful structure of his plot would crash, and he hated to think of the wrath to come.

Nothing of that sort was going to happen—not if Fergus MacTavish could sidestep it. Waiting until Custer was en-gaged in conversation with a patient, the Scot hurried the dog by him, straight to Peter's cot.

"Now, Bran," he whispered. "Here he is—the lad that

saved you. Up wi' you and thank him!" He tugged up on the leash.

He need not have taken all his precautions. Peter had stretched out a hand weakly toward the dog and called to him. Bran knew him at once. Plainly he remembered. The staghound, already standing as high as the low Army cot, rose on his hind legs and put his forepaws on the blanket. Not effusively but with the dignity of his kind, he acknowledged the debt of life he owed this man. He licked the hand that reached around his shoulders.

Moisture shone in Custer's eyes. He spoke the words the dog seemed to be trying to utter.

"Soldier," he told Peter, "he's saying, 'Master, you saved my life, and I'll guard yours with mine as long as we both shall live.' "

6: THE DESERTERS

THE PRISONER

I

Most dogs, symbols of loyalty, will not lightly transfer their
allegiance from one master to another. Some never will.
There are tales of dogs which have taken post on the grave of
an owner and, refusing all food, lain there until they followed
him into the hereafter. But the great majority, after a period
of bewilderment and mourning, will attach their affections
anew. Their need of human companionship is too great to

be long denied. That bond, formed thousands of years ago when the first lonely wild dog crept out of the shadows of a forest and joined a fur-clad man by his fire, holds fast still.

MacTavish realized that he must now break the tie between himself and the staghound, hard though it came, and let Peter become Bran's master in fact. Persuading Peter to accept the dog as his own had not been difficult. Not only was the young soldier eager to protect a comrade in the ranks from the certain wrath of Custer if the General discovered the trick that had been played him; Peter was also proud to possess so fine an animal. But MacTavish understood that only by absenting himself from the scene for some time could the transfer of Bran's allegiance to his new owner be successfully accomplished. Accordingly, he took a furlough to visit his sister in Canada while Burkman, the orderly in charge of Custer's horses, assumed care of the pack also. The Scot waited until Peter was discharged from the hospital, then turned Bran over to him and left the post.

Bran greeted his new master, wagging his tail with friendly reserve. Later he accepted his food from him. Although for days the dog was sad, and his eyes roamed everywhere in search of the Scot, he followed the young soldier who made much of him.

The short remainder of Peter's company punishment was remitted and he was detailed as trumpeter. Bran accompanied him to the outskirts of the post, whence trumpeters were banished for practice, to spare the ears of the rest of the garrison. While in the 4th Cavalry, Peter had been expert but he had not touched the instrument since. As he began to blow again, the first few calls rippled off in fine style—thereafter he was not able to sound anything without a series of discordant blasts and *whooshes*. Like every horn-player, he must toughen his lips, and that was no short, easy task. Bran stayed with him through the days of that process when every other creature shunned the vicinity. The dog sat on his haunches and emitted only a few doleful howls when the trumpeter's attempts to reach "G's" ended in dismal bleats and wails which sounded like the shrieking of a lost soul, nor could his master blame the staghound. Musical practice should be among the most secluded of rites. Peter recalled in sympathy some recent highly uncomfortable moments of his own. During his illness the band had picked the neighborhood of the hospital to practice the "Funeral March" until ordered away by the irate surgeon.

As a trumpeter, Peter found that the color of the mount assigned him was pre-determined. In accordance with an old cavalry tradition, Custer mounted his field music and band on grays and whites. Peter drew an off-shade white, an aging but amiable animal named Humpty. Humpty was slow and short-coupled; when he cantered, he rocked like a hobby horse. Peter's cavalryman's heart was disgusted. No greater contrast to the fast black Morgan, Justin, his mount in the Fourth, could be imagined; but privates in the Army, like beggars, can't be choosers.

Slowly but reluctantly Peter began to fit himself perforce into the Seventh. It was, as the recruit depot corporal had assured him, a good outfit. Custer had given it pride in itself, *esprit de corps*. But Peter was quick to learn, through the enlisted men's grapevine, that in one vital respect it was a house divided.

There was never a more dashing commander in the Army than George Armstrong Custer. *Beau sabreur,* hard-riding cavalryman, he seemed cast in the mould of the great leaders of horse of all time. Yet you either hated him or you loved him—there was no middle ground. Peter Shannon thus far could not decide to which camp he belonged. Stern in enforcing discipline, Custer was sometimes impatient, sometimes actually insubordinate under it himself. There had been occasions in the last war when he disobeyed orders, and once not long ago a court-martial had reprimanded him and suspended him from command and pay for having left his troops on an Indian campaign. When he heard that there had been an outbreak of the dreaded cholera at the post where he had left his wife, he had turned over the column to another officer and ridden back hard and fast with a small escort, never resting till he learned Mrs. Custer was well.

"Who is not for me is against me," might have stood as the motto of the Seventh's commanding officer. Suspicions of favoritism were inevitable in a regiment, one of whose companies was commanded by Custer's brother-in-law, Lieutenant Calhoun, and another by his brother, gallant Tom Custer, who had won two Medals of Honor fighting for the Union. Two other Custer relatives would soon join in civilian capacities. And the regiment, like others, knew the perennial cleavage between the West Pointers, headed by Custer, and officers who had not attended the Military Academy.

In barracks Peter heard the story of a still-smouldering scandal which had almost rent the regiment asunder.

At the Battle of the Washita, Custer had struck a big Cheyenne camp at dawn in the dead of winter. When a trumpeter blew the charge, the three columns into which he had divided his troops thundered down on the Indian village at a headlong gallop through the snow.

"How that windjammer got off that call is more'n I can figure," a bandsman told Peter. "Criminy, it was cold! Hanged if Old Curley didn't order the band to play 'em into action like always. Man, we got off just two bars of *Garryowen* when our breaths froze solid in our instruments and we couldn't blow another note."

"But it was a hot fight, I tell yuh," a sharpshooter took up the story. "Braves come boiling out of the wigwams shooting. Cap'n Hamilton, he got it straight through the heart. We rid right over them Injuns. Some squaws and kids got killed by accidunt. I shot one a-purpose and I won't never regret it. She was standing over a little white boy they'd captured, with her knife up. My bullet got her dead to rights but she still had the strength to slash the poor young un to death."

A third trooper related: "I just missed following Major Elliott, and that's all the reason I'm still here. Off gallops the Major with Sergeant-Major Kennedy and thirteen men. I can still hear him shouting, 'Here goes for a brevet or a coffin!' 'Twas coffins they all got—or rather holes in the ground. There was heap more Injuns down the valley. They came whooping up and smothered the bunch with Elliott. We found what was left of 'em later in a clump of tall grass. The rest of us were hard pressed for a while. Sure was a near thing when we began to run out of ammunition. Reckon I'll never forget the sight of Lieutenant Bell bringing the wagons straight through the Indians. Those galloping mules were laying right down to the ground like jackrabbits, and the wagons swaying all over the place. When they got to us with the ammunition, tar on the wheels was blazing up from the friction."

"What we did to them Injuns was plenty," the bandsman resumed. "Seems like they ain't got over it yet. But Custer was smart to get us out of there with our scalps on. When we was clear and our instruments thawed out, what you think we played? *Ain't I Glad to Get Out of the Wilderness.* And was we!"

The old argument raged heatedly again. Had Custer abandoned Elliott to his fate? Some insisted that he had, since he had heard the sound of distant firing and made no move toward rescue. Others argued that Custer had his hands full. If Elliott had run for it when he saw a mass of tribesmen riding down on his small detachment, instead of standing and fighting, he could have escaped. And all agreed the General had done first-rate in extricating his command from the clutches of the several thousand Indians in lower villages by the feint of an attack and then a rapid countermarch of retreat.

"Some of the officers say Old Curley let Elliott and the rest get scuppered when he could have saved 'em easy," the trooper informed Peter. "Specially Colonel Benteen. He's Cap'n of 'H' Company, my outfit, and acting battalion commander. He's all right to soldier under, Benteen is. You've seen him. Heavy-set feller with a red face and white hair. Looks kind of like Santy Claus. Well, Benteen up and writes a letter burning up the General for letting Elliott down. It gets in the papers. Man, does that start a ruckus! Custer has 'Officer's Call' sounded. He tells the lot of 'em he's going to horsewhip the feller who wrote that letter soon as he finds out who it is, and he gives his boots a mean cut with the whip he always carries—just for a sample. Old Benteen looks him up and down, shifts his pistol holster around to front of his belt handy-like and says: 'All right, General, start your horsewhipping now. I wrote it.' Old Curley backs down and gives 'em dismiss."

"Custer backed down!" cried Peter in amazement.

"For once in his life. Hanged if I know what else he could do."

Others chimed in. "It wasn't exactly what you'd call the beginning of a beautiful friendship." . . . "Them two hates each other's innerds."

Well, Peter reflected, there were bound to be clashes of personalities and interests in any regiment, just as in any civilian organization. The tight discipline of the Army and the narrow confines of a post simply pointed them up. He bitterly remembered Corporal "Hay" Rick in his former troop, "K" of the 4th Cavalry. He and Rick had tangled from the start, and at the last Rick, deserting, had shot and nearly killed him and his mount, Justin.

The Seventh had deserter trouble, too. There were the "snow-birds," men who enlisted in the fall to secure food and shelter for the winter, then cleared out at the first sign of spring. Ever since gold had been struck in the Black Hills, soldiers from every regiment in the West had been turning up their noses at the poor pay and hardships of the Army and taking off to try their luck digging yellow wealth from the ground. That the Seventh should suffer from such desertions was natural, for when the gold rush began, and prospectors and settlers flooded into the Hills, violating the treaties reserving those lands to the Sioux, it had been Custer and his regiment who were ordered out to protect the intruders. Envious troopers watched civilians strike it rich.

Ever since the gold discovery, it was easy to guess where soldiers were heading when they deserted from the Seventh. Consequently, when the report was made one morning that there had been a guardhouse break during the night, the General despatched a pursuing detachment in the direction of the Black Hills.

He barked sharp orders at Godfrey, officer of the guard. "Get after them fast. They've got a good head-start. And bring them back—dead or alive!"

The lieutenant saluted and dashed for the stables on the double. As his sergeant began mounting a detachment, the officer shouted at Peter:

"You, too. Saddle up. I need a trumpeter."

II

Peter found it good to be in the saddle and out on the plains again, and there was tingling zest in a man hunt. He would have much preferred it if this one had been an Indian chase. There was a certain grim unpleasantness about going after deserters—like a policeman having to arrest old neighbors. Sometimes you felt sorry for a poor fellow, driven by some sort of desperation to "go over the hill," but usually deserters were treated with the contempt they deserved. These were men who had broken their oaths faithfully to serve the United States—men who let down their comrades in the ranks. They were malingerers, gambling cheats, thieves—sometimes murderers.

Riding close behind Lieutenant Godfrey, Peter heard him outlining the situation to the sergeant.

"Seven of them," the officer was saying. "There's a couple of horses missing, so two of the deserters are mounted. Maybe more—they may have stolen other animals from a ranch or stage station. If they did, we'll never catch 'em. Our only chance is that some are still footing it. They'll hold back the mounted men if they're sticking together."

The officer turned in his saddle to glance to the rear. "What's that?" he demanded. A small dust cloud was rapidly overtaking them. "Confound it, a dog! Must be one of the General's. Never knew 'em to follow anybody but him before. Sergeant, send a trooper to ride that dog off and get him started home."

"I'll go, sir," Peter offered. "Sorry, but I'm afraid that's my dog, not the General's. He's not very well trained yet."

Bran came bounding up and leaped joyously toward his master's saddle.

"Send him back," the lieutenant ordered curtly.

"I told you to *stay*," Peter shouted sternly down at the hound. "Back you go now. Go *home*."

Bran, deflated and contrite, turned, his flaunting tail lowered to half-mast. Looking apologetically yet half-hopefully over his shoulder, he slunk away from the column. Yet when it began to draw off, the dog could not resist and came loping up again. The age-old, oft-repeated struggle between a man and the dog he is trying to send home was played through. Persuasions were as futile as angry scoldings and chases. Finally Lieutenant Godfrey said: "Save your horse, Shannon. Let the dog come along. Might turn out to be some help."

And so he proved to be. Late that day Bran, who had been running off to one flank, came racing back to Peter. The dog kept uttering short, low barks until he caught his master's attention.

"Sir, my dog smells something off there," Peter reported to Godfrey. "May be only stray calf or a coyote, but it's something alive."

"Can't see a thing but it might be out of sight down in a buffalo wallow," Godfrey declared. "Ride over and take a look."

Bran led the way, quickly out-distancing Humpty. Peter saw the dog slow down, then halt and stalk forward. But investigations were brought to an abrupt halt. Smoke puffed from the edge of the wallow, and a bullet pinged past Peter's head. He wheeled Humpty and spurred back.

The men hidden in the wallow had made a break for it and were a quarter of a mile distant before the detachment could be gathered in for pursuit. Three of the fugitives were seen to be mounted, the rest running beside them, holding to stirrup leathers. They were the deserters, plus an extra man, evidently a plainsman they had picked up as guide.

Lieutenant Godfrey called to Peter: "Trumpeter, sound 'Recall.'"

The deserters paid no attention to the clear notes floating across the prairie.

"Blow 'Halt.'"

The two imperative notes only seemed to hasten the pace

of the pursued.

"All right, Sergeant." The officer needed to say no more. The veteran non-com had handled deserters before and was taking no chances. Once, bringing in a tough character caught going over the hill, he had stopped at a hash-house in town for a meal. Suddenly the man had flung a handful of red pepper straight in his eyes. Blinded and in agony though he was, the sergeant had groped his way out of the door, fired toward the sound of the deserter's footfalls and dropped him. Now he barked sharp orders. Carbines were unslung—breeches clicked open for cartridges, snapped shut. Butts came to rest on right thighs as left hands gathered reins. Carbines at the ready, the detachment took up the trot.

Spurts of smoke from up ahead. The deserters were desperate enough to fight. Godfrey coolly dismounted his men and ordered the horses back. Every fourth trooper, the horse-holder, linked the bridles of three horses to his own, remounted and trotted to the rear, out of range. Men on the line were deployed and commenced firing at will. Prone or kneeling, they picked their targets, and the carbines cracked steadily. Godfrey, shooting also, called out, waved his arm, and the skirmish line moved forward in a rush. They had the range now. One of the deserters was hit, then a second. A horse dropped. The starch went out of them, and a white rag waved from their midst.

Peter, once cease firing had been given, laid down his carbine to grasp Bran's collar. The dog had crouched beside him during the fight but now was becoming difficult to restrain. Preoccupied with him, Peter only half heard Godfrey examining the plainsman found with the deserters. The officer was telling him he kept bad company.

"How'd I know?" the man demanded. "Their story was they'd served their time and been discharged. We met up and they hired me to guide 'em."

"Sounds a bit too pat. Where were you heading?"

"That's my business."

"Where you were taking these men is mine. Better speak up, or I'll have to put you under arrest."

The two men, both still mounted, stared each other in the eye. The plainsman snapped back insolently:

"Arrest me and see what happens to you. Heard of false arrest, ain't you? You got nothing agin me. Outa my way. I'm ridin'."

"Wait! Hid in the wallow with these deserters, didn't you? What'd you think they were hiding for? If they were time-up men, all they had to do was show me their papers. Stuck along with them when they ran and then tried to shoot their way out, didn't you?"

"Sure I did." The other sneered. "One agin seven, wasn't I? Reckon anybody'd have sense enough to shut up and play poker then."

Godfrey reluctantly reined back. "Guess I can't hold you," he acknowledged. The plainsman, nonchalantly dismounting to tighten his cinch, flung back: "Naw, you can't—not you nor any other shave-tail still wet behind the ears."

Peter grinned to himself. He didn't like the fellow's voice and he probably was a bad *hombre* but he had made a neat job of facing down the lieutenant. The trumpeter, still holding Bran, moved over for a better look.

There was something familiar about the set of those shoulders. If they'd been covered by Army blue instead of buckskin—. The plainsman turned toward Peter full face. His reddish beard was not disguise enough. Peter knew those hard eyes, those coarsely-handsome features, the small, weak mouth under the moustache. You remembered a man who had tried to kill you. It was—no doubt of it—his old enemy Rick, former corporal in the 4th Cavalry and carried on its rolls as a deserter.

Lieutenant Godfrey, looking crestfallen, had dismounted and was ordering: "Sergeant, have those seven deserters tied up."

"Make it eight," Peter shouted. "This bogus plainsman's a deserter from the Fourth!"

III

Things happened so fast Peter could only sense them at the moment and had to reconstruct them afterwards.

Recognizing Peter, a malevolent glare flashed in Rick's eyes. The deserter knew he would not be able to talk his way out of this one. A leap, and he was in his saddle—the only man mounted in the group. Soldiers scrambled for weapons, out of reach or emptied in the recent fight, or dashed for horses. Rick squandered two precious seconds of hatred on Peter. He reached for his pistol, forgetting he had been disarmed when he was taken prisoner. Next he gathered his mount to ride the trumpeter down.

Bran exploded a menacing growl, rising on his hind legs and tugging madly against the collar his master still held. Rick took one look at the furious dog and swung his horse to one side. The animal plunged against the officer's mount and bowled it over. Rick rode straight through the horse-holders, making them drop reins and scattering their charges. Random shots fired after him went wild.

Peter watched the fleeing figure grow small in the distance. In the years since that moment in Texas when Rick's bullet had grazed his skull and "creased" Justin, Peter had often wondered what he would do if ever they met again. Well, he had done next to nothing—only denounced him and let him get away. Should he have loosed Bran? No, that would only have exposed the young hound to a kick from Rick's horse or the thrust of a hidden knife.

What was done was done. Rick, branded as a deserter both in the Southwest and now in Dakota Territory, would make himself exceedingly scarce. Like Indians of the Plains tribes, defeated on the warpath, he would ride north to safety over the Border. Odds were a hundred to one that Peter ever would face his enemy again.

7: A PLACE IN THE PACK

CALL TO QUARTERS

I

The veteran cavalry horses, many with five years of service and some with ten or more, knew the trumpet calls as well as or better than their riders. Their ear for music was keener than that of many a trooper who depended on comrades or his two company trumpeters to identify calls. Of their own accord, grazing horses ambled back to stables when they heard "Recall" sounded. During drill some scornful steed, bored with the rookie bumping about on his back, would toss him off and, riderless, nonchalantly obey every signal sounded.

Dogs on the post were equally musical. As quickly as a

master's whistle, they recognized various trumpet calls. Favorites, of course, were "Mess Call" and the flourishes blown by the Custer brothers on hunting horns. Yet the dogs seemed to be familiar also with all the calls of the long succession that timed the regiment's day, from "First Call" for reveille through "Taps." Peter claimed that when he was trumpeter of the guard, Bran reminded him when to sound off.

But there was one call the young staghound had not yet answered—the call of the pack. At first he had been kept apart through necessity, because he was being hidden. Later Peter had segregated him to make certain nothing distracted Bran from knowing him as his master. But the time was at hand when Bran must respond to a canine "Call to Quarters," when he must find and join the pack.

Late one afternoon, while his master was on duty, Bran slipped away and trotted over to Officers' Row. The pack, just fed by Burkman, was lolling in contented ease behind General Custer's quarters. Lazy old Lucy Stone was dozing. Bran's mother, Maida, was asleep inside on her rug. The pointer Ginnie, Eliza's favorite, thumped her tail as she dreamed. Byron, the lordly greyhound, lay couchant, as if posing for an heraldic crest. Other greyhounds and foxhounds—Brandy, Rattler, Jupiter, Sultan, and Tyler— napped or scratched. Turk, Tom Custer's stubby white bulldog, was about to saunter off and join his boon companion, Phil Sheridan, one of George Custer's chargers, named after the famous general who had been Old Curley's beloved leader in the war with the South and who now commanded in the West. The bulldog and the horse were the closest of friends. When Turk reached the stall, Phil and he would rub noses and exchange snorts of affection. A playful nip at the slim legs, and strong equine teeth would grasp the scruff of the dog's neck and lift him over to his bed under the manger.

In dignified repose the staghounds gazed off into the distance—Tuck, Custer's particular pet, Blucher, Lady, and various youngsters. Their ears pricked up and they swung their heads to watch the door. Their fellow, the cream-colored Cardigan, was making an undignified exit from the house, impelled by a vigorous push from Eliza's broom.

"Pesky, sassy ol' houn'!" the cook scolded. "Big, ol' good-for-nothin', you won't never learn. Thinks you is a lap dog, does you? All the time climbin' up on po' Miss Libby's lap, and you twice the size she is. What she do? I declare she go piece herself out with a chair so she kin hol' you. And what you do, you big, ol' elephunt? You jes' lies there and lies and lies. Bye and bye her po' laigs goes asleep. Houn', does you care? Not you, you's asleep, too. Miss Libby, she jes' sit and hol' you till she cain't stan' the pricklin' in her laigs no mo'. She say so sweet, 'Oh, Cardigan, please move.' Then Eliza comes a-runnin' with the broom. Now git!"

Cardigan sailed off the stoop, with the most comically sheepish expression imaginable. He half lit on one of the other dogs but there was no other resentment than a low growl, for Cardigan still bore the scars of a recent fight in which he had given a good account of himself.

It was at this moment that Bran approached the pack.

II

Uncertain of his welcome, Bran advanced slowly, his tail wagging a little in a deferential and ingratiating manner. Yet there was nothing cringing about him; he was a dog of consequence and he knew it. He had won a name with the regiment on the deserter chase. The Seventh, not his master alone, was proud of him, and officers and enlisted men spoke to him and patted him.

But his reception by the dogs was another matter. At once he sensed that he was confronted by their traditional unfriendliness toward a newcomer. Most of the dogs rose and bristled. It took courage to go ahead. Bran's walk slowed still more and he stalked forward on stiff legs. It was like the new boy coming to school for the first time. Naturally it was toward the staghounds he made his overtures. The older hounds remained aloof—not so one of the younger ones, one of Bran's own brothers. No human being could have told whether they knew their relationship. If they did, brothers, canine or human, can be quarrelsome.

The one-time weakling of the litter was now closely matched in size and strength with this brother named Lufra. Rumbling deep in their throats, the two stood muzzle to muzzle and traded insults. Suddenly Lufra emitted a ferocious growl and reared up on his hind legs. Bran rose to meet him. After the manner of staghounds in combat, they grappled like wrestlers. The fight was on.

The tumult, with all the pack joining in, barking and yipping, reverberated along the Row. Windows opened, and back doors framed spectators. Prisoners policing up the post found work which demanded their immediate presence in the vicinity and hurried over, willingly accompanied by their guards. Women called out pleas to stop the fight, but nobody seemed to know how to go about it. Neither General nor Mrs. Custer, who had gone for a walk, was home, nor was any officer in sight.

Bran and Lufra tangled in a mêlée of tawny yellow and reddish hide. As excitement infected the pack, a large foxhound jostled Turk. Instantly the white bulldog leaped for his throat, and a second battle was joined.

Turk clamped on his grip, that deadly hold for which the bulldog was bred and trained and named. For seven hundred years his breed had used it in the cruel English "sport" of bull-baiting, fastening it on the nose of a bull—breathing easily through their own snubbed noses—hanging on no matter how wildly they were swung about—at last dragging their mighty adversaries to the ground. Turk's teeth inched in further along the neck of the frantic foxhound, slowly strangling him.

An officer, Tom Custer, came running up. He seized his bulldog's hind legs and tried to pull him off. Turk held on the tighter. Only when his master grabbed a carbine from a guard, slipped the barrel under Turk's collar and twisted it did the choked dog release the gurgling foxhound.

Meanwhile the young staghounds stood clawing and tearing at each other. Neither was able to gain any advantage. Blood dripped from their jowls and from deep gashes in their shoulders. This fratricidal strife would end only in crippling wounds or death, for the tenacity of the staghound is no less than the bulldog's. Back and forth they wrestled, towering on their hind legs nearly as high as man. Soon one of these splendid animals must die. Captain Custer was busy with the other fight. No soldier was willing to risk a bite from those slavering jaws. A guard did move up to club the pair apart with his gun but thought better of it; he would have to strike so hard he might seriously injure one or the other. Most of the spectators showed no desire to interfere. Hardened, facing death or disablement in the ordinary course of their own calling, these frontier troopers wasted no sympathy on the fate of the struggling dogs. An ancient blood-lust gripped them, that same fierce thrill which seized the crowds in the Roman Colosseum watching combats of animals, or their English forebears at a bull-baiting or badger draw—a frenzy which even at that moment in American cities and towns cast its evil spell on men and boys crowded around secret, illegal pits where matched terriers or mastiffs tore at each other.

Suddenly Lufra reared up on his hind legs. Bran rose
they grappled like wrestlers.

to meet him. After the manner of staghounds in combat,
The fight was on

Civilization and mercy were sloughed off as the stag-hounds' conflict neared its climax. Entreaties screamed by women from the windows of quarters went unheeded. Watchers hoarsely cheered the combatants on.

"Go git him!" "Chaw him apart!" "Five dollars on the red un!" . . . "Take yuh!" . . . "Sic him, Fido!"

Staghounds bark sparingly. Except for rasping growls, deep in their throats, the two fought in silence. Now Bran made mighty thrusts forward with all the power of his haunches. Gradually the other dog was borne back. In a moment they would go down, with Bran on top, giving and taking terrible wounds till the finish.

A rush, and two blue-clad figures pushed between the combatants. Peter and MacTavish, returned from furlough, had arrived only just in time. Each man took bites on hands and arms from the infuriated hounds but they succeeded in separating them. Stern commands sent the two fighters crouching to earth, panting.

The crowd had melted hastily away. Peter and MacTavish began washing and salving the dogs' wounds after Eliza had helped them attend to their own bites. Now that hostilities were over, the staghounds paid no further attention to each other. The Scot grinned and remarked:

"Do ye ken Bobbie Burns, young Shannon, the grandest poet in Scotland or the world?"

"Yes, some of him. 'Tam o' Shanter' and 'Auld Lang Syne.' "

"I'm minded now of 'The Twa Dogs.' " Scotty quoted:

> " 'When up they gat, an' shook their lugs,
> Rejoic'd they were na men but dogs;
> An' each took aff his several way,
> Resolv'd to meet some ither day.'

" 'Tis so wi' Bran and Lufra," he continued. "They're na like men who have fought to kill. They'll bear nae grudge, these twa. Most dogs willna—'tis only the few that fight on sight whenever they meet."

"Does look like there are no hard feelings." Peter stroked his dog's head. "Bran," he ordered, "there'll be no more scrapping. You've fought your way into the pack. You belong now, old boy."

8: NEW LOYALTIES AND OLD

MAIL CALL

I

AT SUNRISE and sunset the old field piece on the parade
ground of Fort Abraham Lincoln boomed its daily salute
to the Stars and Stripes, hoisted up the flagstaff to unfurl
in the prairie breeze, or lowered for the night into the waiting arms of a color sergeant. As acrid fumes curled from the
gun's vent, Peter thought: "That's the only powder I've
smelt, except for the deserter chase, since I've been back in
the Army."

But unmistakable signs pointed to action. Sooner or later
the Seventh must take the field against the Sioux and
Cheyennes whose young braves were jumping their reservations more and more frequently, to gallop off on raids.

Charred ruins of cabins and the scalped and mutilated bodies of settlers marked their path. In a few weeks the savages would return to the reservation, all innocence, to draw their rations of Government beef and flour and demand more ammunition for their repeating rifles "for hunting."

Occasionally detachments of blue-clad troopers were sent to round up the raiders and herd them back and sometimes they accomplished their mission. As often, the redskins escaped over the Canadian border, where they could not be followed, only to come whooping back again at will. It was a sorry state of affairs which could not be allowed to continue. Settlers, paying even less regard to treaties than the Indians, were demanding that the Government furnish protection, and the Army would be ordered to strike. Not much longer would small punitive expeditions hold in check the fighting Cheyennes or the fierce warriors of the Sioux nation, for years tyrants over the lesser plains tribes. From Washington would come orders mustering a sizable force to crush the Indian menace once and for all. And in that force the 7th Cavalry surely would ride.

Preparing for the reckoning to come, Custer drilled his regiment mercilessly. Under Lieutenant Cooke, forty picked sharpshooters, excused from guard and fatigue details, trained the less accurate shots on the target range. More recruits and remounts arrived.

Peter, although Custer's taunt about transferring from the Seventh with a campaign ahead still rankled, had written his friend, Major Lindsay, adjutant of the 4th Cavalry, asking him to put in for him. Very probably the Fourth had plenty of fighting in prospect, too. He could not understand why he had not yet received an answer, nor why the Major's daughter, Sally Ann, had not written him for weeks. It might be that her letters, forwarded from the East, had gone astray, but it was more likely she was preoccupied with all her officer beaux. He thought bitterly: Fickleness, thy name is woman. It's out of sight, out of mind with her. Absence makes the heart grow fonder—of someone else.

His face was red when he responded to "Mail Call" one day. With a grin and considerable ribbing, the mail orderly dealt him out a missive in a familiar rounded handwriting, postmarked from an Army garrison in New Mexico. He ducked behind barracks to read it in private, while Bran, obviously sharing his joy, sat on his haunches and regarded his master fondly.

Peter dear (it read): How *perfectly marvelous* you're back in the Service!!!! Honestly, I *knew* you couldn't stay out for long.

First thing, I ran right over to stables to tell Justin about it. Remember, you told him you'd be back. Pete, cross my heart I vow he *understood!!* He put his soft nose against my cheek and nickered. He sends his love, too.

Peter could not contain his emotion. So she hadn't changed, after all. The letter sounded so like the little girl he'd begun to love that night down in Texas when she came up to tell him how well he'd blown "Taps" and presented him with a package of cookies. Eagerly he read ahead, half skipping an irrelevant and irritating paragraph about goings-on at the post. Sally Ann's pen flowed on:

When I rushed over to Headquarters to tell Dad you'd re-upped, it was no news to him. There was a letter from you on his desk, military as anything, saying the 7th Cavalry had snagged you in spite of your putting in for us, and you *simply had to* get back to the Old Fourth. Pete, if you didn't want to, I'd NEVER FORGIVE YOU!!!!

But listen, Peter, the Seventh is a good outfit, too. General

Custer is *simply wonderful* and Mrs. Custer is so sweet. Now just stand fast and hold your horse a while, soldier, and see how things work out. You know as well as I do it doesn't do a trooper any good to kick up a big fuss with the C.O., and I do so want to see you win a commission from the ranks.

So what do you think I've done? I *practically ordered* Daddy to put your application for transfer down under all the papers in his basket!

"Young lady," he booms, "do you venture to delay an action which is in the best interests of the military service?"

"Sir," says I, "what's a few months in military channels which are slower than molasses anyway?"

So, Peter, if you don't hear anything for a while, you'll know why. My word is practically Pop's law.

Write soon to your best girl (I hope I *still am!!!!!!*)

Sally Ann

P.S. This letter sounds like a schoolgirl's, and I'm a grown-up young lady, but I *am* so glad you're back in the Army.

Peter dropped the letter with an expression of such baffled bewilderment that Bran gave a little moan of sympathy. Angry resentment surged up in him. The nerve of the girl! What was she getting at, anyway? So she wanted him to stay here and win a commission. Didn't she care anything about him unless he was wearing epaulettes? Maybe there was some young officer she was crazy about down there, and this was just a preliminary to her handing him, Peter Shannon, the mitten.

Write her? Not he! What he would write would be another letter to Major Lindsay, requesting immediate favorable action on his transfer to the Fourth.

II

When you are down in the depths of the blues and your thoughts tangled into knots, hard work is the best anodyne. Peter, knowing that, flung himself into the Seventh's preparations. His lips had toughened up, and Chief Trumpeter Hardy, who had ridden behind Custer through the War Between the States, praised his new man's trumpeting and stationed him in the front ranks when the field music was massed. As Adjutant Cooke had observed, martial music was dear to Custer's heart and he used it with telling effect in garrison and field. Chief Musician Felix Vinatori, with the warm blood of Italy in his veins, led the band with fire and *bravura*. His sixteen bandsmen, mostly German, responded with ringing harmonies. Ever memorable to Peter was the day he first passed in review with the regiment while the band blared the rollicking strains of the march the Seventh had adopted as its own, *Garryowen*.

That march, its lively six-eight tempo ideal for cavalry, had been suggested by Captain Myles Keogh, one of the company commanders. Keogh, once a Papal Zouave and a veteran of hard fighting in Africa and our own war, had learned it in his native Ireland from his father, member of a Royal Irish Lancer regiment. On pay days the Lancers consorted at Owen's Garden, a tavern for which their song was named, to roar out its chorus over foaming tankards of ale. It was ironical that the Seventh's march, originally a drinking song, should have been introduced by Myles Keogh, himself the victim of a raging thirst. That officer drank up his pay as fast as it was doled out to him by his striker, to whom he had handed it over, since he could not trust himself not to spend every cent of it on whisky. Change the words of *Garryowen* here and there, and it was just as appropriate for the Seventh's wild pay day sprees as for the Lancers'.

Garryowen.

Lively.

1. Let Bac-chus' sons be not dis-mayed, But join with me, each jov-ial blade; Come booze and sing, and lend your aid, To help me with the cho - rus.

Chorus.

In - stead of Spa we'll drink down ale, And pay the

reck - 'ning on   the nail; No   man for debt shall

go   to jail From Gar - ry - owen in   glo - ry.

We are the boys that take delight in
Smashing the Limerick lights when lighting,
Through the streets like sporters fighting
And tearing all before us.

We'll break windows, we'll break doors,
The watch knock down by threes and fours;
Then let the doctors work their cures,
And tinker up our bruises.

We'll beat the bailiffs out of fun,
We'll make the mayor and sheriffs run;
We are the boys no man dares dun,
If he regards a whole skin.

Our hearts so stout have got us fame,
For soon 'tis known from whence we came;
Where'er we go they dread the name
Of Garryowen in glory.

Yet Peter, passing in review to *Garryowen*, seldom
thought of its words. He glanced over at Captain Keogh,

riding his stocky bay charger Comanche at the head of his company. Sober, he was a fine soldier. As the band played, Peter was caught up by the stirring panoply of the march past.

Gallant in Army blue, the companies sat erect in the saddles of their matched mounts, following the national and regimental standards, majestically outflung, and the fluttering cavalry guidons of red and white. Good men and nondescripts. War veterans and raw recruits. A former brigadier general of volunteers in rank beside a lad fresh from the farm. Scores of troopers who once had worn the gray of the Confederacy, like Peter's comrade of the Fourth, Lance Elliott, killed by Chief Quanah in Texas. Some of these had been captured while the War Between the States still was in progress and released from Northern prisons to fight the Indian tribes, with the promise they would not serve against the South. They were called "galvanized Yankees" because iron, when galvanized, changes color as they did the hue of their uniforms.

Custer, five loops of gold braid glistening on his sleeves, took the salutes. Past him with his squadron rode swarthy, saturnine Major Reno, inexperienced in Indian-fighting but the bearer of three brevets for gallantry in action in '61–'65. Benteen, sweeping up his sabre and commanding, "Eyes right," returned the General's narrowed gaze with a scowl. On with their companies came Tom Custer, grinning at his brother; Captain Yates, and young Lieutenant Trelford, also blond and handsome. Captain Smith managed his reins in spite of a crippled left arm. Keogh swung by, and two other former Papal Zouave officers, Nowlan and De Rudio. Yonder stood out the bronzed aquiline features of Lieutenant Donald McIntosh, half Indian, half Scot. There rode merry Benny Hodgson, Varnum, his boon companion, and other able young West Pointers, Godfrey and Hare, who one day would don general's stars. That was Jack Sturgis, son of the Seventh's colonel who was on detached duty and, to Custer's delight, never had appeared to assume command of the regiment.

As he watched—no mere spectator but a part of it all— Trumpeter Peter Shannon struggled against an unwelcome sensation: pride in a regiment he never had meant to call his own.

III

Only a few favored troopers could gain access to the Custer kitchen out of the many who tried. Eliza's cooking, which could completely disguise Army rations as savory dishes, was a potent lure indeed. Once a soldier, weary of the monotonous slumgullion and beans of his company mess, had tasted of Eliza's art, he never stopped trying for another sample until he had exhausted every wile and trumped-up excuse in his bag of tricks.

MacTavish and Burkman, as Custer's orderlies, were privileged characters in the kitchen. In fact, the latter had been feasted there for weeks at Mrs. Custer's orders. That good lady, told by the surgeon that Burkman was threatened with lung trouble and should have especially nourishing diet, instructed Eliza to stuff the horse orderly full of food, whether he wanted it or not. But Burkman's co-operation was nothing short of hearty. He ate himself out of his decline and kept right on after he had recovered. As a result, he was known throughout the Seventh as "Old Neutriment."

Since the day he broke up Bran's fight, Peter had often returned to the Custer quarters, knowing he would find his dog with the pack company in that vicinity. It must be admitted that few of his trips were necessary; Bran usually would come back to barracks of his own accord, but

Peter, like others, knew the Custer kitchen and its culinary charms. On several occasions the General had sent Peter in to get a meal after a late detail had made him miss regular mess.

Craving more of the same, Peter laid a plot, prompted by MacTavish. Dropping over for Bran after Retreat, the trumpeter found Eliza seated on the back-door steps, enjoying the fine spring evening.

"Eliza," he remarked casually after a greeting, "I often wondered how you happened to come to work for the General."

That, MacTavish had assured him, was the Negro woman's favorite story. Once warmed by telling it, she would hand out everything on the stove to a good listener. If she did not rise to the bait this evening, it would be too bad for Peter, who had gambled heavily on it by passing up mess.

Eliza looked a trifle suspicious but could not resist.

"Well, young sojer, it happen like this," she began. "It happen back in '63, down South with the fightin' goin' on all aroun'. All the darkeys was excited over freedom, and I craved to see how it was. After the 'Mancipation, everybody was a-shoutin' for liberty, and I wasn't goin' to stay home when the res' was goin'. Day I come to a Union camp there was lots of other darkeys standin' roun'. Ginnel come up to me and ask my name and I tol' him Eliza. Ginnel he looks me up and down and ask would I like to come and cook fo' him. I looks *him* all over and sez, 'Reckon I would.'"

She had worked faithfully for the "Ginnel" ever since— under fire in the field, through dire hardship on the plains. Now she rose to go back into the house. "Miss Libby say dinner be late 'cause company's comin'. Things jes' sp'ilin' on the stove. Couldn't git nothin' anyway from the Commissary 'cept canned tomatoes and peaches. And beef—all the time beef. I declare I'se et so much beef I 'spects to grow horns and beller."

Peter laughed loudly in appreciation. "That's a good one, Eliza," he praised.

Eliza said: "Vittles jes' sp'ilin' on the stove. Young sojer, you got appetite enough for a bite while they's hot?"

The schemer and base flatterer thought he could manage.

Peter had risen from the "bite" in repletion and was thanking Eliza profusely when wheels rattled out front. The late company was arriving. He heard General and Mrs. Custer's voices in happy greeting and responses in feminine tones. That would be one of the pretty girls from Monroe, Michigan, the Custers' home town—one of the belles they often invited for a visit to gladden the hearts of all the young officers of the regiment. Evidently one of them was being gladdened already, for Peter recognized the voice of Lieutenant Trelford, who must have acted as the young lady's escort. The General's voice cut through.

"So she's practically engaged, is she, Libby? Hurrah! Then we won't have to order the officers to propose by platoons."

"I think they will anyway, Autie," came Mrs. Custer's answer.

"I," Trelford put in gallantly, "am first and foremost."

Peter smiled at the girl's gay laugh. As he moved toward the back door to depart, he caught her rejoinder: "No decision can be taken, Lieutenant, till I've gone out in the kitchen and asked the advice of my old friend Eliza."

Tread of light footsteps. Framed in the doorway like the lovely picture she was stood Sally Ann.

IV

No wonder he had not recognized her voice. It held maturity, a deep-reaching thrill he had not known. In two years she had become a grown-up young lady [as she had written]. Her wide, hooped, brown traveling dress was caught up into a fetching bustle. A saucy little hat, adorned with feathers, perched forward at an angle on her chestnut curls, most of them swept back into a chignon confined in a snood. But the same clear, candid gaze looked out at Peter from her hazel eyes, and her little nose still was freckled and wrinkled a trifle across the bridge when she smiled.

"Peter!" she cried—then faintly, "Oh, Peter."

He was sure she was coming straight into his arms, but she glanced at Eliza and only ran forward to put both her hands in his. They stood there, speechless, gazing deep into each other's eyes.

Eliza, arms akimbo, watched, beaming. "It's jes' about time," announced the cook. "I declare I was gittin' ready to leave this heah wilderness an' desert fo' good and all. Ain't been no picnics, no church sociables, no burryin's—an' no weddin's. Now reckon mebbe Eliza stays."

Sally Ann blushed. She and Peter both began talking at once. Now didn't he see why she'd urged him to stand fast with the Seventh? . . . Yes, but why did girls like to make a fellow suffer for weeks? She ought to have written she was coming to visit the Custers. . . . Didn't men ever like a nice surprise, or wasn't she one? . . . . "Gosh, Sally Ann, you're prettier than ever, and gosh, how I've missed you!"

The click of spurred boots interrupted them. Lieutenant Trelford stood watching them, a puzzled, a distinctly annoyed expression on his handsome features. Peter took in the tall, lithe figure in the dashing uniform and knew the contrast with his own shorter stature and plain trooper's garb was no happy one. He snapped to rigid attention.

"Trumpeter," Trelford declared curtly, "the General says for you to take my mount back to stables and turn him over to my striker. And tell them at the junior officers' mess I won't be there. I'm staying to dinner."

"Very good, sir." As he left, Peter saw the lieutenant
offer his arm with the gesture of a cavalier and Sally Ann
take it with a smile.

9: THE BARRIER

THE GARRISON BELLE

I

INVISIBLE but solid as a lofty stone wall stood the barrier of rank, dividing enlisted men from officers. Some officers built it higher and more impenetrable than it was ever intended to be. Old and embittered martinets or green lieutenants, uncertain of themselves, they issued orders like petty tyrants or slave-driving overseers. Others—fortunately in the great majority—exercised command in the true tradition of American armies which began when the Minute Men mustered at Lexington and Concord. For them and the men they led, the barrier denied neither mutual respect nor comradeship.

When Peter joined the 4th Cavalry as a youngster, he had accepted the wall and all its implications without question. A trooper must take his officers on trust—and they, likewise, their superiors in rank—for they were all "set under authority," like the Roman centurion in the Bible. Peter vividly recalled that story from St. Luke's gospel, told him by his officer father one day when they had been talking of rank. How the centurion's servant, who was dear to him, had fallen gravely ill, and the commander of a hundred had appealed, through the elders of the Jews, to Jesus to heal the dying man. Jesus was on the way to the Roman officer's house, when the centurion sent friends to meet him, saying:

"Lord, trouble not thyself, for I am not worthy that thou shouldest enter under my roof. Wherefore neither thought I myself worthy to come unto thee; but say in a word, and my servant shall be healed.

"For I also am a man set under authority, having under me soldiers, and I say unto one, Go, and he goeth: and to another, Come, and he cometh: and to my servant, Do this, and he doeth it.

"When Jesus heard these things, he marvelled at him, and turned him about, and said unto the people that followed him, I say unto you, I have not found so great faith, no, not in Israel.

"And they that were sent, returning to the house, found the servant whole that had been sick."

As it was in the Roman army, so must it be in the American. A soldier had to render his officers faithful obedience. It was authority, justly exercised, and the discipline it enforced that marked the difference between an army and a mob. And to command most capably an officer must keep himself a little apart and avoid that over-familiarity which breeds contempt. Neither Peter nor most of his fellow-troopers would have had it otherwise. R.H.P.—initials mentioned often in the Army—meant: Rank has its privileges. True, but it also imposed its responsibilities. The ability to lead those who loyally followed. The duty of seeing to your men's welfare before your own. The hard compulsion upon a commanding officer of sending soldiers to face death in battle.

But that scene in the Custers' kitchen had upset Peter considerably. Rank seemed to have altogether too many privileges with Sally Ann. It was plain enough that Lieutenant Trelford and the rest of the young officers would be monopolizing her. She was a young lady now and he, Peter, still a trooper. Gone forever were the days when they were youngsters together in the Fourth, and Peter and the pert tomboy of a girl had ridden together and danced at the "K" troop hops.

Peter saw now why Sally Ann was so insistent on his trying for a commission. That was a hard path, with veteran officers still applying and a new crop of shavetails from West Point every year, but it could be traveled; in fact, it had been achieved in the Seventh. Lieutenant Moylan, who had been the regimental sergeant major and a corking good one, had come up from the ranks. Custer had backed him every step. When the newly-made lieutenant had been barred by a snobbish group from the junior officers' mess, the General had confounded them by inviting Moylan to become a member of his own household.

And Peter soon saw that Sally Ann had no intention of neglecting him. Ordered to escort her—and Mrs. Custer—on a morning ride, Peter saddled Humpty and, his heart beating fast, fell in behind the ladies. No sooner were they out of sight of the post than, in response to a smiling gesture from Mrs. Custer, evidently admitted to the secret, Sally Ann dropped back to ride beside the trumpeter.

"Peter, where did you get that wonderful white hobby horse?" the girl called with her old gay impudence. "Listen, I didn't have a chance in the kitchen to tell you about Justin. He's just grand, the darling. Pete, I swear he misses you. Every now and then I catch him looking for you wistfully."

"Gosh, I miss *him!* But he's your horse now, Sally Ann."

"Yours, too, Pete. I promise you."

Out of a dust cloud Bran loped up and leaped over Humpty's rump.

"Thought I told you to stay home," Peter chided the dog. "But now you're here, I guess you can stay. We can do with a scout like you in case there are any stray Indians around."

"What is that perfectly gorgeous creature?" Sally Ann demanded.

"He's a staghound and he's mine." While the girl leaned from her saddle to pat the dog's fine head, Peter told her Bran's story. They were chattering away like old times when Bran signaled the approach of horsemen from the post, giving Sally Ann time to ride up beside Mrs. Custer. Shortly Peter recognized the riders as Captain Tom Custer and Lieutenant Trelford. He frowned grimly, all his happiness dispelled. This was the way it was going to be.

II

Trelford immediately ranged his mount beside Sally Ann's. The party broke into a canter, and Peter, wincing with jealousy, noted how admiringly the lieutenant watched the girl's superb horsewomanship. Tom Custer had joined his sister-in-law but his eyes were busy roaming over the ground.

Watching for rattlesnakes, Peter surmised. The prairie swarmed with them and it was well to avoid those poisonous reptiles, lying torpid in your path or coiled ready to spring. However, they were not very dangerous to anyone mounted; your horse spotted them and gave them the right of way. Even men on foot were seldom fatally bitten, although a rattler could throw itself about three times its length from a coil. Boots and the heavy cloth of breeches were some protection, and recruits were instructed on treatments to use if bitten. One questionable panacea was downing all the whisky the victim could lay hands on. Better methods were the application of ammonia or black mud from the sun-baked surface of a buffalo wallow, or cutting the wound open to let it bleed and persuading some comrade without any abrasion in his mouth to suck out the venom.

Few were free of a certain amount of dread of rattlers, with their penchant for crawling into a man's blankets at night for warmth. But Captain Custer seemed fond of them; he collected them. As inclined to pranks and teasing as his brother, he seized any opportunity to play on the fears of poor Elizabeth Custer.

Now he sighted a quarry, a big snake with ten rattles or more. He swung out of the saddle, pulling his carbine from its boot. Peter also dismounted and grasped Bran by the collar; he would not risk the young hound's being bitten. As Tom approached, the rattler coiled, and its tail vibrated with warning clicks. Tom laughed and tempted it to spring. It launched itself at him like a javelin. He stepped back, and the reptile fell just short of his boot toes. Before it could coil again, he dexterously pinned its head to the ground with the butt of his carbine. He bent down, grasped it behind the head and picked it up writhing, then walked over with it to Mrs. Custer, who cringed in her saddle and drew back trembling.

"Well, old lady," he said with a grin, "I have a beauty to show you. Caught him just for you. Here you are."

Sally Ann cried out. "Oh, Colonel, don't!"

Tom roared with laughter. "Aha!" he shouted. "I've been rudely neglecting a guest. I apologize. This beauty is all yours, Miss Lindsay. Here, I present him to you."

He walked over, thrusting the rattlesnake's menacing triangular head straight at her. Its forked tongue darted out between its fangs, as it twisted and squirmed in his grasp.

Sally Ann turned white. With a rapid motion, she drew a little derringer from beneath her blouse and shot the snake right out of the officer's hand.

Tom stood there, his arm still extended, his mouth gaping, and an expression of such stupefied amazement spread over his face that Peter burst out in loud guffaws and shouted: "Hurray for you, Sally Ann!" No sooner had he spoken than he bit his lip, but the words were out.

Lieutenant Trelford cast him a curious and angry glance.

"That will do, Trumpeter," he ordered sharply. "Return to the post. We will escort the ladies."

III

A man's dog is a great solace in time of trouble. Since the episode of the rattlesnake shooting, when Peter had given himself away, he had spent all his off-duty time with Bran. He did not dare even to visit the Custer kitchen for a glimpse of Sally Ann. Every officer in the regiment, he knew, was toasting and making much of the girl. They had christened her Calamity Jane II and declared she would wing a man with as little compunction as that famous frontierswoman and mule-skinner. Tom Custer now vied with his juniors as Sally Ann's devoted admirer.

Peter occupied himself in training Bran, encouraged by MacTavish, who was aware of his friend's depression. The Scot told him tales of the great hounds of legend and history. Of Fingal's Bran who hunted with a pack of one thousand and for every stag captured by others Bran brought down three. Of Help and Hold, deerhounds of Sir William Clair, a knight who wagered with his king, his head against a royal manor, that the dogs, swimming across a river in pursuit of a stag, could turn it before it reached the further bank. Fast though they swam, they seemed unable to overtake their quarry. Sir William had resigned himself to death when, only a few yards from the further shore, Help turned the stag and Hold seized him. When the dogs came to the end of their days, Sir William arranged that their likeness be carved in marble, crouched at the feet of his own effigy on his tomb.

MacTavish told, too, the tale of Llewellyn's famed hound, Gelert. When the chieftain returned from a hunt, he found his dog, left on guard at home, covered with gore. Rushing in to see if anything had happened to his infant son, Llewellyn saw the babe lying in his overturned cradle, also drenched with blood. Certain the hound had slain the child, he stabbed Gelert through the heart. Only then did he discover a huge wolf under the bed, killed by the hound in defense of the babe, who was unharmed. Ever since, the place where the hound was buried with honor has been known as Beth Gelert, Grave of the Greyhound.

In barracks Bran always slept beside his master's bunk. It amused Peter to watch the staghound settling down— how he followed the habit transmitted to every dog from his wild ancestors, circling around and around before curling up to sleep, as if hollowing out a bed for himself in the fallen leaves of a forest.

MacTavish called over from his own bunk. "Next winter

you'll be glad of yon hound. You ken it grows bitter cold on the plains. When we're out on a scout and under canvas, Bran will be better than any stove. He'll lie close beside you and keep you from freezing stiff."

Scotty grinned reminiscently. "There's nae few of the officers who make complaint of the Gen'ral's dogs. I'm minded of a tale of one of the worst complainers. 'Twas last winter, wi' the regiment tenting on the plains in a blizzard. Icy cold it was and sae far below zero there was nae counting degrees. Yon officer comes shivering to the Gen'ral to beg a dog to warm him and gie him a guid night's sleep. He gets a big hound. Aye, it warms him well enough but it couches on the officer's chest, twitching wi' dreams of chasing rabbits and snoring lounder'n the officer. Next night he comes back to change it for a sma' dog that didna snore."

"Some officers are never satisfied," Peter remarked with more than a trifle of bitterness.

But he was well aware as he tossed in his bunk that every officer in the regiment was more than satisfied with Sally Ann.

IV

In the 4th Cavalry, her father's outfit where she had grown up, Sally Ann was the daughter of the regiment. Although she never had lacked attention there, here in the Seventh she was fervently courted as the garrison belle. It was different, and she loved it.

Many a girl from the East, making her first visit to a western post, was dazzled by gold braid and the glamor of Army life. Young officers vied in teaching the newcomer to ride and shoot, and the frequent sequel was a bride on a blue-clad arm, walking under the traditional arch of crossed sabres.

To Sally Ann the Army was an old story but nonetheless a beloved one. She had been reared in the Service—an "Army brat," as the saying went for Army children. None of the Seventh's lieutenants presumed to instruct her on horses and firearms after the expert demonstrations she had staged. They did try to trick her one day when a quartermaster wagon, drawn by a six-mule team, came rolling by the porch of the Custer quarters, where Sally Ann was holding court for half a dozen beaux.

"Hold up there, teamster," Jolly Benny Hodgson called to the trooper driving. "We have a relief here for you." The wagon halted, the teamster setting his brakes and climbing down.

"Now, Calamity Jane the Second, let's see if you can handle mules like Jane herself," Benny invited Sally Ann.

Without a second's hesitation the girl rose. Gathering up her skirt, she allowed willing volunteers to help her up on the seat. Then she grasped the reins competently in her small hands, released the brakes and shouted like a veteran muleskinner:

"Now you lop-eared, splay-footed, old hay-burners, move out! *Hup!*"

Sally Ann, cracking her whip, drove the team out on to the parade at a fast trot. She took the mules around at a full gallop, completely disrupting a squadron drill. Trumpeter Shannon watched goggle-eyed, as he rode behind the squadron commander. He blew "Countermarch" instead of "Right wheel," and the entire formation broke into a milling mass. Sally Ann drove back to the Custer quarters and pulled up amid wild cheers.

Peter unsaddled, groomed, watered and fed his mount in grim silence, smarting under Benteen's rebuke for mixing his trumpet signals. What was the matter with the girl, making a spectacle of herself like that? Turned into a show-off—that's what she'd done. Major and Mrs. Lindsay wouldn't like her carrying on like that a bit. It was his duty, as an old

Sally Ann took the mules around at a full gallop, completely disrupting a squadron drill

friend of the family, to speak to her. Besides, he hadn't seen her except at a distance for days.

Eliza welcomed him in the Custer kitchen. Sounds of merrymaking penetrated from the parlor. That was Sally Ann's clear young voice lifted in song, accompanied by the chords of her guitar and the twanging of Tom Custer's Jew's-harp. Peter caught the rollicking strains of *Buffalo Girls*.

> *I asked her would she have a dance,*
> *Have a dance, have a dance.*
> *I thought that I might get a chance*
> *To shake a foot with her.*

Hearty male voices roared out the chorus:

> *Buffalo gals, ain't you comin' out tonight,*
> *Ain't you comin' out tonight, ain't you comin' out to-*
> *night?*
> *Buffalo gals, ain't you comin' out tonight*
> *And dance by the light of the moon?*

Sally Ann swung into another verse.

> *I'd like to make that gal my wife,*
> *Gal my wife, gal my wife.*
> *I would be happy all my life,*
> *If I had her by my side.*

Wouldn't they though! Any man jack of them, confound them! Eliza's kind black face puckered in sympathy, as she noted Peter's deeply downcast look.

"Jes' you wait," the cook told him.

Eliza slipped into the parlor but was soon back.

"She seen me but seems like she won't take no notice," Eliza reported sadly. She bustled over to a cupboard. "Made me pie today," she announced. "Cut you a slice, young sojer?"

"No, thanks, Eliza. I'm not hungry."

"Got a nice batch of cookies."

Cookies! Bitter memory. Peter could only shake his head. Disconsolately he pushed out into the night.

10: OFF THE RESERVATION

TATTOO

I

"TATTOO," sounded by two trumpets, floated across the parade ground through the spring evening. Peter, his skill returned, was helping a green trumpeter of the guard blow the long, beautiful call, a favorite along with "Taps" and the "Call to Quarters." He explained to his pupil, as he had learned in his own apprenticeship, that "Tattoo" or "Taps to" originated in Europe's Thirty Years' War, when its notes warned tavern-keepers to close the taps of wine casks and serve no more to hard-drinking troopers. Now it had become a signal to duty sergeants at barracks to call the roll of their platoons and report all present or accounted for, or to note any absentees who might have overstayed their passes in a misguided and unavailing attempt to drink up all the liquor in the Bismarck saloons.

The tempo of "Tattoo" was quick, and the new wind-jammer needed Peter's support on the low "C's" toward its close. As it died away, Peter's spirits lifted. Tomorrow he might be sounding off in action. He had been detailed to ride with the detachment Custer was taking out to round up a band of Sioux who had jumped their reservation.

Only two companies, Calhoun's and Keogh's, mounted up in the morning. This was no more than a preliminary to the big campaign for which the Seventh was preparing. A supply wagon, loaded with extra ammunition and rations, swung in behind the cavalry; it would be left under guard if need arose for fast movement to catch the fugitive Indians. Custer also took along some of his pack, with a view to hunting game as he rode. No foxhounds were included; they were better for the winter hunting in underbrush and timber and they were apt to be too noisy. Custer chose a half dozen of the greyhounds and staghounds and gave Peter permission to take Bran.

Several dogs that might have gone were left home as a punishment. They had indulged in an early morning chase after a "prairie dandy," as polecats were called because of their handsome black and white markings. The little animal had routed them with his tried and true defense. When the reeking hounds came bounding back to the Custer quarters, sure of their usual welcome, they were driven out with sticks and chairs by their master and mistress and the wrathful Eliza. Mrs. Custer peeped out the door to watch them sitting in a grieving semi-circle, questioning their short treatment with little whines and wagging apologetic tails to beg for reinstatement. MacTavish led them off in disgrace.

With the two companies formed in column of fours, the cavalcade rode across the plains, fresh with the breath of spring. Scouts fanned out ahead of the advance guard. Custer in buckskin, his long yellow curls streaming from under his broad-brimmed campaign hat, red bandana around his sunburned neck, galloped far to the left flank. The pack strung out after him. Back among the slower dogs, Peter pounded along on Humpty. Bran, who might have raced in the van, was content to run at his master's side.

It ran through Peter's mind: Put a red coat—"pinks" they call 'em, don't they?—the color of that bandana, on the General, and he'd be the picture of a smart Master of

Hounds, with me as one of his Whips on a slow cob. Anybody would think we were hunting a fox, not Indians.

The illusion became still more vivid when the hounds spurted off after a jackrabbit. It was the swift Tuck, vying with the greyhounds, that seized the quarry and trotted back to Custer with it in his mouth.

The General waved his trumpeter forward and handed him the rabbit with a grin of pride. "It takes a fast dog to catch a jackrabbit," he declared. "And who says a staghound isn't a good retriever? Tie this long-eared fellow to your saddle, Shannon, and give him to the cook first chance you get. He'll flavor the stew."

Custer rode on at a walk, resting the dogs. Half to himself, half to Peter, riding to his left rear, he commenced talking.

"These Indians we're after—they're only one bunch of lots who'll be jumping the reservation this spring. By summer most of the Sioux nation will be out. The Cheyennes, too. Trust old Chief Sitting Bull and Crazy Horse for that.

"Can't say I blame 'em," Custer mused. "It's now or never for 'em. They know the sands are running out for their people. We're hemming them in everywhere. On the plains we're killing off the buffalo—the Indians' livelihood. We've taken the Black Hills, theirs by a treaty we made with them. No wonder they turned down the Government's measly offer of six million dollars for the Hills. They know about all the gold being mined there.

"General Sheridan says the Indians are destined to be crowded out. It's a fate they can't escape. It's what has always happened, all through history, when a strong, civilized people has moved in on nomad tribes.

"So the Army gets orders to herd the Indians back on their reservations. Naturally they don't want to go. Too many of 'em are rotting and starving there, with the Government's Indian agents grafting on their rations. I tell you, the trail of corruption leads so close up to the White House that—"

The General broke off suddenly. Those were words an enlisted man should not be allowed to overhear.

His mood altered swiftly. The dogs were off on a second chase. Whooping, Custer galloped after them at full speed. This time it was a big gray wolf. He led them three-quarters of a mile before he turned at bay. The kill was a mother-and-son performance. Heedless of the beast's terrible, slashing snaps, Maida and Bran dashed in savagely and seized him. Peter heard their jaws crunch his bones. The wolf disappeared under a mass of growling hounds.

Lieutenant Calhoun galloped up. "Good riddance!" he said. "I remember a time we were camped out—you were away on leave, General. I was officer of the guard, and my good wife was alone in her tent. Maggie woke up in the middle of the night, with some animal beside her cot, sniffing at her. She thought it was one of the dogs and offered it a piece of hard tack. The animal snatched it out of her hand and ran. Outside the tent one of my sentries fired. Maggie looked out at the body of a big timber wolf like this fellow. She's never felt hospitable toward any of your dogs at night since, General. They might be a wolf in disguise and Maggie says she's through playing little Red Riding Hood."

Custer laughed and ordered camp made.

Horses were watered, fed, groomed and picketed. Bacon and coffee cooked over the fires. Troopers, mess over, lay around, smoking their pipes. Peter questioned his friend, Sergeant Ellis, a veteran of long service whose dragoon's mustache was tinged with gray. The trumpeter asked him about the graft by Indian agents of which Custer complained so bitterly.

"There's plenty of it, all right," Ellis affirmed, "and it's rotten, though there's some honest agents. But the crooked ones get away with it. Government pays 'em a salary of about fifteen hundred bucks a year. In about four years they retire with $50,000 or better in loot, made out of grub and clothes supposed to be issued the Injuns.

"No wonder the Injuns bust loose. I see their side of it. But you forget it quick enough when you see what they've done to some trooper in your outfit they took alive."

"Yes, I saw that in Texas," Peter answered grimly.

"Or what happens to a white girl they capture," Ellis went on. "She wishes she was dead before they get through passing her around from chief to chief, with jealous squaws making her do all the work and beating her black and blue all day. I've seen those girls afterwards. The Seventh has rescued some of 'em."

The Sergeant's words seemed destined for quick confirmation. Next morning, when the detachment rode up to a cabin, a settler, rifle in hand, faced them across his broken-in door.

"Bunch of Sioux rid' in yesterday," he announced laconically. "I was out of the house. Saw 'em from the draw yonder and was scairt to move. Robbed the place but didn't burn it somehow. When they rid' off, they took my daughter with 'em."

II

With action in prospect, Custer galvanized a command like an electrical current. He snapped out a string of orders. Troopers stuffed extra rounds of ammunition and two days' rations into their saddlebags and swung into saddles. The wagon was left behind, guarded by a squad of cavalrymen whose horses were used up. No more wolf hunting now—

the quarry was fiercer game. Dogs, whining in protest, were collared and tied to the wagon wheels, but Custer left three free: Blucher, Tuck and Bran. Those sturdy staghounds could keep up.

Custer's eyes gleamed with pride in his hard-riding troopers. They made better than twenty miles that day, and halted for a few hours' sleep in the starlight. Charley Reynolds, the reliable old scout, had ridden on far ahead. An hour before dawn he galloped back to report:

"They're up thar, Gen'ral. Fair-sized village. Might be as many as a hundred braves, with their women and childrun. All quiet. Reckon they got hold of some liquor on raids, and they're sleepin' it off."

Custer listened with satisfaction, sitting his saddle with the look of an eagle about to swoop down on his prey. The shadowy figures of Keogh, Calhoun, and their lieutenants gathered around the General to take his crisp, decisive orders. The prelude to the Battle of the Washita was to be enacted again, with Custer dividing his force in that favorite maneuver of his and hitting the enemy on all sides.

A quiet-spoken command, and the troops moved out. There were no sounds save the beat of hoofs, the creak of saddle-leather, the grunt of a horse here and there. Sabres, whose clanking might betray, had been left at the post.

Reynolds, riding beside the General, spoke softly. They were drawing near the Indian encampment. Custer's upflung right arm, faintly discernible in the fading starlight, halted the cavalcade. Smoothly it separated into four columns which rode off into the darkness to encircle the village. They were in position before the stars winked out in the first glimmer of the coming dawn.

Custer turned to Peter and lifted a hand. The stirring, staccato notes of "Charge" blared across the prairie. Troop trumpeters echoed it from the other three points of the compass. The four columns converged at a gallop, guidons snapping in the van. Again the trumpets sounded. "Left front into line." The rear squads obliqued, spurred and pounded abreast of leading squads. A two-rank cordon swept in as if it were a string drawing taut the mouth of a sack. Peter saw one platoon detached to cut out the Indian pony herd. Lines deployed and closed the gap.

A pack of howling Indian dogs came boiling out of the village in full cry. One look at the three staghounds, and the mongrels fled yelping, tails between legs. So close on their heels rode the blue cavalry that sleepy Indians, snatching up weapons and bursting out of tepees, found themselves surrounded and covered. They stared sullenly into the muzzle of leveled carbines ringing them around, dropped their rifles and bows and hoisted their hands. Not a shot had been fired.

The band's chief stalked up to Custer and asked him to smoke the pipe at a parley.

"No talk," Custer snapped. "You're prisoners, and we're taking you right back to the reservation. But first hand over that white girl, you carried off, and if you've done her any harm, you'll pay for it! Where is she?"

The scowling chief pointed. "She in my lodge there."

The General dismounted. "Lead the way," he ordered and strode alone after the chief. Captain Keogh ran after them, making a protest.

"Sir," he begged, "let me take a squad into that lodge first and clear the place out. Might be an ambush."

Keogh knew Indian trickery. There might be half a dozen Sioux inside, and they would have a splendid opportunity to knife the General, once he entered. Keogh had seen more than a few skirmishes when attacking warriors had broken and galloped off in retreat when their chief fell. Likely enough this chief figured that the loss of their leader would have the same effect on the soldiers, and the band could then turn on their captors and rout them.

But Custer, brave to the point of rashness, ignored the precaution his company commander urged. He flung an order over his shoulder for the troops to force the Sioux to break camp, pack up and be ready to travel in fifteen minutes. Followed only by the three dogs, Old Curley walked calmly up to the tepee and disappeared inside. Its flap closed behind him. Outside the staghounds stood guard, bristling. No Indian dared approach within ten feet of them.

Peter watched Bran with pride. The young staghound was thrice the size of any of the Indian curs. Probably the red men originally possessed bigger and better breeds, for they had owned dogs when the white man first invaded the continent, and those animals then had served as their only beasts of burden. When war steeds, brought over by the Spaniards, fell into the hands of the Indians, or escaped and bred wild herds, horses supplanted dogs with the savages for pack and draft. More important, horses served the tribes as mounts, with the result that the plains Indians became the superb cavalry they now were. Dogs, no longer as essential, had degenerated into camp sentinels or a source of food. They were not even widely used for hunting any longer. The red man on horseback, with his marvelous skill in trailing and stalking, had little need of canine aid.

The speed and efficiency with which the Indians broke camp, hastened by an occasional shove from a carbine butt, fascinated Peter. In a matter of seconds the tepees were struck, the squaws doing most of the work. The tepee poles, bound one on each side of a pony, with a crosspiece or two, formed the travois frame. On that the buffalo hides which had been the shelter's wall, were loaded, along with buffalo robes, blankets, kettles, and other gear. Squaws, some with papooses strapped to their backs, climbed on the ponies.

Small children and old people perched themselves on travois. Now bare, the camp-ground presented a scene of dirt and squalor. Indians never troubled to clean up when they were moving on to another site for the next night—or even when they were not.

When General Custer emerged from the council lodge in exactly fifteen minutes, the entire band was in readiness to take the trail. He beckoned Keogh, who hurried up.

"Take over, Captain Keogh," Custer ordered. "Form your men up on both flanks and in rear of the prisoners and head for the reservation. Move at once. I'll follow directly."

The mouth of the Irish soldier of fortune gaped. Was the white girl inside the lodge? How many Indians were in there beside the chief? What in thunder was the General up to, anyway?

Keogh's mouth clamped shut. He opened it only to utter, "Yes, sir." He saluted, knowing better than to oppose Old Curley twice.

Custer ducked back inside the lodge and dropped the flap.

The two companies of cavalry, escorting the Sioux, rode off, leaving the camp with its one tepee still standing. In every flabbergasted officer and trooper bubbled emotions in which curiosity and apprehension for the General were mingled.

Peter spared a glance back. The three staghounds still stood guard outside the lodge. That, at least, was reassurance.

III

Keogh, worried, kept the column at a slow walk. In any event, the prisoners could not move much faster, and they, too,—so far as one could read their impassive faces—looked puzzled and ill at ease. Their chief could not be regarded as any too safe in the company of the formidable Yellow Hair, as the Indians called Custer. The white leader might come galloping up flourishing a black-haired scalp.

A mile, then another and another, was covered. At last came the sound of pounding hoofs. Through their own dust cloud, escort and prisoners sighted the Sioux chief overtaking them at a trot. After him rode his squaw on a pony hitched to a travois. The vigilant staghounds bounded along on either flank. Custer brought up the rear. There was no sign of the white girl.

As the Indians joined the other prisoners and Custer rode on to the head of the column, Peter thought that his commander's countenance, which never tanned but reddened under the sun, was more crimson than usual. The trumpeter was ordered to sound "Officers' Call," and the commissioned personnel galloped up to ride in a knot around the General. Troopers saw that he was recounting what had happened and that the officers were drinking it in with amazement. Not until the halt for noon mess did it filter down through the grapevine to the rank and file.

Custer, as soon as his eyes became accustomed to the dim light of the lodge's interior, had seen the settler's daughter seated on a buffalo robe. Back in the shadows behind the chief sat a third figure. Instantly on his guard, Custer demanded of the chief:

"Who's that there? Speak up."

"Him friend. Trader," the chief identified the other man.

Probably a half-breed or a squaw man, then. Many such were the scoundrels who were selling the Indians firearms and liquor. Little could be done about them unless you caught them red-handed. Custer turned back to the girl.

"Are you all right?" he asked, scanning her carefully.

She stared back at him brazenly. Custer took in her bold good looks. "Certainly, I'm all right," she answered.

"We came along fast, soon as we found your father at his cabin and heard the Indians had you," the General declared. "I'm glad we were in time."

"Weren't no hurry," she remarked. "I got treated fine."

Custer regarded the chief with a quizzical frown. "So much the better for you," he told him. Then he addressed the girl again. "All right, Miss. We'll take you back home on our way to the reservation."

"Won't be troublin' you," she answered shortly. "I'm stickin' with my trader friend here."

"No," Custer decided. He had managed a plainer survey of the figure in the background and was not in the least prepossessed by him. "Guess you'd better come along with us, Miss."

The settler's daughter flared up. "You're not givin' me orders. I'm free, white and twenty-one, I am. I tell you, I've stood all I'm a-goin' to of that old devil of a paw of mine. Works me to the bone, he does, and never lets me have no fun." She nodded toward the trader. "Him and me's goin' to get married."

Nothing Custer could say had any effect. It was useless warning this woman that a man she had picked up with a day ago was likely to abandon her as soon as he tired of her and that, probably, would not take long. The argument ended with her "sassing" the General in language that was far from ladylike and daring him to stop her.

Custer controlled his impulse to force her to return home. What a fine spectacle he would make, riding up to his troops holding a biting, scratching, kicking hussy in front of his saddle. There was a good chance, too, that if he used force, the trader would put a bullet in him from behind.

General Custer knew he was beaten. With such dignity

as he could manage, he let the couple go, ignoring broad grins on the faces of the chief and the trader.

Custer had told that story on himself to his officers, chuckling at his own predicament.

At the noon halt, Trumpeter Shannon was surprised with a summons to report to his Commanding Officer.

"Shannon, you've heard about what happened in the lodge?" the General began.

"Yes, sir. Happens I have."

The General burst out laughing. "The grapevine is the most reliable system of communications in the Army," he avowed. "But there's something that happened toward the last I can't understand. It was that hound of yours, Shannon. He's a good dog. Didn't he tear into that wolf the other day, though! But I've never known him to act hostile toward anybody in the outfit or any dog—except, of course, that scrap with Lufra, and that was a fair fight. Well, when we came out of the lodge, hanged if Bran didn't go for that trader fellow with fangs bared. I tell you, Bran was going to take him apart then and there. I managed to get a grip on his collar, and it was all I could do to hold him."

"I can't figure it out, sir," Peter said. "Never knew him to do anything like that before. Wait! There *was* a time. That time we went after the deserters and— Sir, did that trader have red hair and a beard and—"

"Sure he did!" Custer exclaimed. "I've got it. He was that deserter from the Fourth you reported. The man that tried to ride you down, and Bran scared him off."

"Yes, sir. It must have been Rick, all right. He was smart, staying inside the tepee so's none of us who'd seen him before could spot him."

"Like to lay hands on him," the General snapped. "But it's too late now. He and the girl have a long headstart. The chief let 'em have a couple good ponies.

"Shannon," he finished, "we'll take that staghound of yours along whenever we're likely to run into any rascals or renegades. As surely as he knows his friends, a dog remembers his enemies."

11: TO BEAT THE BAND

FULL DRESS

I

PETER and MacTavish were getting into uniform for one of the dress parades which Custer was fond of staging for dignitaries visiting Fort Abe.

"'Fine feathers make the bird,'" Scotty quoted sententiously, regarding his gala getup with distaste, "'but fine clothes dinna make the mon.'"

"You don't like the new full dress, Scotty?" Peter asked. "Me now, I think it really tricks out the regiment and makes a grand show." He polished brighter the gilt eagle blazoned on the front of his black-laquered helmet, copied from the British Horse Guards. From its spike streamed a horsehair plume, dyed cavalry yellow. Frogged braids of the same hue spanned the chest of his dark blue tunic; on its arms were sewn the "stripes and bugle" of his rank. The buckle of his sabre belt, his scabbard, and his high boots and spurs glistened in the sun pouring through the barracks' windows. The twin yellow stripes of a trumpeter ran down the sides of his breeches, which were of lighter blue than the tunic. On his cot lay white gauntlets and his trumpet, whose cord repeated the cavalry color.

"I dinna like it," the Scot declared flatly. He quoted again, this time from his favorite, Bobbie Burns.

> "O wad some Pow'r the giftie gie us
> To see oursels as ithers see us!
> It wad frae monie a blunder free us,
>   An' foolish notion:
> What airs in dress an' gait wad lea'e us,
>   An' ev'n devotion!' "

"Some pow'r did give us that giftie, Scotty," Peter pointed out. "Take a look at yourself in that mirror." He indicated a fragment of looking glass affixed to the wall. "Won't anything satisfy you Scots but plaids?"

"Ay, tartans." Scotty glowed. "Ay, I'd gladly don them again. Kilt and sporran. Blue bonnet on my head and claymore at my side and the folds of the long plaid ower my shoulder. Mind you, nae gaudy tartan like the Buchanans' or Ogilvies', but a braw, bonnie ane like the Campbells' or the MacArthurs'."

"Or the MacTavishes'."

"Ay, sin' you mention it. But as I said, 'tis the mon beneath that matters. Does the color of his coat make a dog? Wi' a staghound, there's many a mon that claims a coat of dark blue-gray is the bonniest. Ithers prefer dark grays or brindles or red. Bran there's a guid sandy yellow, yet were he white— a color few like in a staghound—you'd look far to find his equal."

"No argument on that, Scotty."

"Nane at a'. Leave fine feathers to the birds, say I. They have guid reason for it. 'Tis by their plumage they attract their mates."

"That, Scotty," said Peter, finishing dressing, "is such a good reason that what I say is, Why leave it to the birds?"

Resplendent in full dress, he strode out to the parade ground, hooking up his sabre and shifting his trumpet to the carry under his left arm. There was still twenty minutes before assembly. He might meet Sally Ann.

II

For once, Peter told himself, I can stand up beside that glorified shavetail, Trelford, and not feel like the fellow that wore his working clothes to the party where everybody else was dressed up fit to kill. He's taller than I am and a lot better looking, but in dress uniform he can't put me in the shade. He sports gold braid where I've got yellow worsted, with some loops draped over his manly bosom, but that's all—except those blamed epaulettes on his shoulders.

Peter sighted Sally Ann strolling along the edge of the parade ground. For a wonder, she was not surrounded by officers and she had detached herself from a group of ladies waiting to watch the review. It was marvelous what an Army woman out on the frontier, who seldom or never had a chance to visit New York shops, could do when an occasion called for gay apparel. She took long, thoughtful looks at plates depicting the latest Paris fashions in a copy of

Harper's Bazaar which had reached the frontier months late. Then she went to work on a bolt of satin or her year-before-last best gown, and the result was extraordinarily becoming, as Sally Ann now demonstrated. She was attired in a creation of Lincoln green. A smart Eugenie hat with plumes of darker green crowned her chestnut curls. Over one shoulder she carried a small and virtually useless but infinitely fetching parasol.

Peter, pretending to be engaged in some important duty, touched the brim of his helmet, as he hurried by.

"Halt," called Sally Ann. "About face. What's all the rush? Going to blow the 'Call to Arms,' are you, Trumpeter?"

"I know somebody who wouldn't answer it, if I did."

The girl blushed vividly. "Pete, you're mad at me," she charged. "And I know why. That other night at the Custers' when Eliza peeked in, I just couldn't leave the company. I slipped out soon as ever I could but you'd gone."

"You were having too good a time."

"Just how do you expect me to act? Would the Custers ever invite me again if I moped around in my room all day and spent every evening in the kitchen? I hate not seeing you more, Peter, but isn't this a lot better than you being in New Haven and me 'way off in New Mexico?"

It was all perfectly reasonable, but Peter, jealous and unhappy, was beyond reasonableness.

"No, this is worse. It's just tantalizing, having you so near and never seeing you, except once in a while by accident, or on the sly. It's no use, Sally Ann. An enlisted man hasn't got a chance. It's better if we just forget each other. 'By. I'm due at the stables."

"Oh, Peter, wait! You don't mean that. Come over to-night. There's a party, but I'll get a headache and beg off and slip out to the kitchen. I've got to hear about that roundup of the Sioux and how that awful Rick turned up again—and lots of things."

"Sorry but I'm on duty."

Sally Ann stamped a small foot. "I don't believe you!"

"Don't then."

"Oh, Pete, let's not quarrel." Sally Ann's brown eyes, which had been flashing, grew tender. "Do you realize how handsome you look in full dress?"

"Thanks. Even without any epaulettes?" There was gruff, biting sarcasm in his tone.

Peter knew he was acting unpardonably. He could not seem to help it. Having spoken, he was too stiff-necked to retract his words. Anyway, best end this affair before he was given the mitten, as he inevitably would be.

He raised a hand to his helmet in farewell. But he faced only a trim, indignant back and the expanse of a little green parasol which seemed to say, *"That* for you!"

III

A trumpeter was a long way from being a commissioned officer, yet, Peter consoled himself, he was a considerably more important figure than a buck private. He was the "Captain's hitching post," as the Army saying went, always close at hand to hold his commander's mount, sound his calls and carry his messages on the battlefield. He was a fighting man, too, as Peter himself had gallantly proved in combat with the Comanches on the Staked Plains of Texas. And nothing could launch troops into action like the martial blare of the trumpet, sounding "Charge" or "Rally."

Peter's old friend, First Sergeant Sam Smith of the 4th Cavalry, former professor and ex-major of Volunteers, once had told him a tale apropos of the effect of the trumpet: old Aesop's fable, "The Trumpeter Taken Prisoner."

A trumpeter, being taken prisoner in a battle, begged hard for quarter. "Spare me, good sirs, I beseech you," said he, "and do not put me to death without cause, for I have killed no one myself, nor have I any arms but this trumpet only."

"For that very reason," said they who had seized him, "shall you the sooner die, for without the spirit to fight yourself, you stir up others to warfare and bloodshed."

Moral: He who incites to strife is worse than he who takes part in it.

Peter recalled with pleasure that for once he had been prepared with an adequate retort to the learned Sam.

"All right, Sergeant, all right," he answered, "but do you happen to remember that passage in the Bible about how Gideon smote and conquered the host of the Midianites with only three hundred men? All three hundred of 'em, so says the Good Book, were trumpeters!"

The trumpeters of the Seventh, who were to ride massed in the review today, assembled and stood to horse. They breathed into their instruments to warm them, making little guttural snorts and limbering their lips. Today they would display a clever musical device, adopted by Chief Musician Vinatori. Since only five notes can be sounded on the trumpet, several players were provided with trumpets in different keys. The men furnished with these only blew notes which would have been sharps or flats in the key of the majority of the trumpets and hence not in their range. Thus the field music was able to play scores which otherwise could only be performed by the cornets, clarinets, and trombones of the band.

Yonder where the band had fallen in, Adjutant Cooke, whose responsibility it was, made an anxious, last-minute inspection. Trouble could all too often be expected from bandsmen; they were temperamental musicians. They were always trumping up excuses to get out of fatigue details, claiming that they had to practice. That, of course, was true—practice made the difference between a good band and a terrible one—but frequently bandsmen were caught during practice periods taking their ease and puffing away on nothing more musical than a pipeful of tobacco. Cooke agreed heartily with Adjutant Charles King, of the 5th Cavalry, who wrote stories about Army life. King in one of his pieces had demanded:

"Was there ever a band that did not contain among its talented musicians some irreclaimable devotees to Bacchus? And, as a rule, aren't the bandsmen apt to be the most fractious and unruly set in the garrison? Music, that hath charms to soothe the savage breast, by some strange freak of nature, develops an unhallowed taste for beer and a distaste for discipline among its chosen disciples, and rare indeed are the instances when the guardhouse is not graced by the presence of some prominent instrumentalist, usually the snare-drummer." And King had gone on to tell of an uncomfortable occasion when his colonel had summoned him to complain: "This morning my breakfast was one-half hour late, and when I sent to the kitchen to hurry it up, there was my cook, sir, sitting on your bass-drummer's lap."

But Cooke, accompanied in his inspection by Vinatori, could find nothing out of order in the Seventh's band this afternoon. When it was mounting up, the bass-drummer's horse had acted skittish but that was quite as usual. That animal, boasting as much temperament as any musician, tried to emulate a bucking broncho and throw his rider until the drum was strapped on his back. Once it was aboard, and the horse Whitey had been assured that it was indeed there by several deep booms thumped out on it, he became as calm and contented a steed as anyone could ask. Obviously the bass-drum was his pride and joy, and without it Whitey simply refused to be imposed upon by any man.

Drummer Jenks, who had been tossed off too often for his liking, took pains to let the horse know that the drum was among those present on the hurricane deck. If his steed ever grew sceptical while the band was not playing, the drummer tapped the drumhead gently to reassure him and play safe.

The review commenced. As usual the Seventh acquitted itself nobly. Squadrons passed at walk, trot and gallop to spectators' applause. The massed trumpeters gave a spirited rendition of *That Little German Band*. Vinatori's bandsmen took over in their turn, not only a treat to the ear but a spectacle for the eye on their matched white mounts. Some instruments were furnished with rings for little fingers, so that the musician could hold them and operate the valves with one hand, while guiding a horse with the other. Cornets and trombones blared. Tuba and bass contributed sonorous oom-pahs. The snare-drummer tapped out rapid-fire rolls, flams, and paradiddles. The bass-drummer punctuated with such magnificent booms that all Whitey's doubts were resolved and he stepped out, supremely confident that he was carrying the most important instrument in the band.

They played *Inman Line* and *Northern Route*. Next, at the previous request of the visiting dignitary, who had served under Sherman in the march from Atlanta to the Sea, they struck into *Marching Through Georgia*. Every ex-Confederate in the ranks squirmed in the saddle, scowled and muttered under his breath, but visiting dignitaries must be humored.

The music ceased, as the review drew toward its close. That period of silence was chosen by the horse Whitey to be seized with one of his attacks of scepticism. Was the big drum still up there aboard him? He had not heard it for some time. The drummer, sensing his steed's disquiet, produced two or three soft beats. Whitey was not convinced. That man, not always trustworthy, might be fooling him.

Sally Ann took one look at her seated friend's inimitable expression and burst into gales of laughter. "Oh, Peter," she gasped. "You look so-o-o funny!"

He curveted a bit and arched his back.

Drummer Jenks was overwhelmed by sudden panic. Come what may, impending catastrophe must be averted. Better a solitary, unscheduled thump than the sudden conversion of a review into a rodeo, with Drummer Jenks taking the part of a losing contestant in the bucking broncho event. He drew back his stick and hit his drum a mighty wallop.

It happened that the stroke came at the moment when the band, countermarching, was passing the massed trumpeters. The unexpected boom reverberated with a thunder clap that would make the sunset gun sound like a feeble echo. Whitey was satisfied, but Peter's mount, Humpty, only a few feet away at that instant, was startled to within an inch of his life. With a wild squeal of terror, he broke ranks and dashed away.

Peter, sitting his saddle loosely, his melancholy thoughts elsewhere, was caught completely off guard. Humpty ran away with him, skidded to a four-footed stop at the edge of the parade ground and pitched him off in a soaring arc.

Right in front of a knot of ladies, Trumpeter Shannon smote the parade ground with his bottom and a dull thud and sat there.

The best of horsemen have been policed in their time and taken it with good grace as part of the game. But circumstances alter tossings.

Sally Ann rushed forward from the group of ladies. She took one look at her seated friend's inimitable expression and burst into gales of laughter.

"Oh, Peter," she gasped. "You look so-o-o funny!"

Lovely woman stoops to other follies than that with which the poet chides her. One of the most regretable is laughing out loud at a man whose dignity and self-esteem have been profoundly, painfully and publicly shattered.

"So-o-o funny!" Sally Ann chortled again. The words

and laughter were undeniable, irrevocable.

Peter glared up at her. "Oh, do I!" he snapped. Without another word, he picked himself up, ran to where a grinning trumpeter had caught and held Humpty, mounted up and took his place in ranks.

He did not heed Sally Ann's anxious call, "Peter! I'm sorry. You're not hurt?" He tore up, unread, the tearful note of apology she sent him by Eliza.

Sally Ann's headache was a real one that night. She did not come down to the Custers' party but stayed in her room and sobbed herself to sleep.

12: FIRE CALL

Repeat at will

I

THE Custer dogs were despondent. Their once sprightly friend, Sally Ann, seldom played with them any more. Overshadowing her neglect was the abstraction of General and Mrs. Custer, stricken with some serious worry of their own. The pervading gloom was infectious, and Eliza, MacTavish and Burkman shared it.

Unceasingly the dogs strove to distract those they loved.

No human being could have proffered sympathy more plainly. They laid their heads in laps, gazing up and begging with their eyes for caresses. Although they were not altogether ignored, the petting they received was absently given, even by Custer.

For the General was face-to-face with a situation which he knew might prove the most heartbreaking of his career. "Custer's luck," as the Army termed it, seemed about to desert him for once. Ill fortune hit a years-long favorite all the harder. Custer could look back over his career to one lucky combination of circumstances after another. Graduating at the bottom of his class at West Point, he had plunged into the midst of the War Between the States to win victory after victory and climb the ladder of promotion with astonishing speed. After the war, in the review of the Grand Army in Washington, Custer's charger ran away with him. Down the line of march he galloped alone, sitting his horse like a centaur, yellow hair streaming, the very image of martial gallantry. Though critics carped that no horse ever had run away with Custer without urging, the eyes of a nation, already doting on him as one of its heroes, dwelt on him that day. On through the Indian wars, the "breaks" for which every soldier hopes abetted the General's undeniable abilities and fearless leadership.

But now a turn of the tide threatened. Exposures of grafting by Indian agents and post traders—exposures Custer had helped make—had exploded in a national scandal. As the General's soliloquy that day in Peter's hearing had declared, the trail led up close to the White House. Secretary of War Belknap had resigned under fire and barely escaped impeachment by the Senate. Evidence, some of it assembled by Custer, showed that tens of thousands of dollars in tribute money had been paid by traders to higher-ups. President Grant's personal honesty was not shared by some of his subordinates, and the stern efficiency of the one-time Commander of the Union armies had sadly faded in the Chief Executive.

Custer had been outspoken in his accusations. Now he must back them up. He had been ordered to Washington to testify before a Congressional committee on War Department expenditures. As an opportunity to correct conditions which gravely hampered his duties on the frontier, the summons was to be welcomed. But he was well aware that an Army officer who criticizes Government actions risks his career with a certain type of politician. And these orders to leave his post and report in Washington would deprive him of a cherished opportunity.

"Custer's luck." That sounded ironical now. The big campaign against the Sioux and Cheyennes was imminent; in fact, it already had commenced. Despatches informed Custer that a column under General Crook, conqueror of the Apaches, was marching down the Powder River Valley to strike the defiant Chief Crazy Horse. Only bad weather had prevented General Terry from launching other columns, to include the 7th Cavalry.

To be ordered away on the eve of action was more than Custer could bear. He forwarded an earnest request that he be allowed to make sworn depositions of his testimony and remain to command his regiment in the field. Yet he could not rid himself of dire forebodings that his plea would be denied.

Listless, Custer sat on the porch of his quarters. His dogs clustered around him, begging for attention.

Elizabeth Custer watched him with fond concern. His dogs so rarely failed to cheer her husband. Only a few days ago she had written a paragraph in her journal about her Autie and his pack: "I look at the master to see if he realizes that all that is faithful and loving in this world is at his heels.

If he stops to talk to a friend, and one of his dogs leaps about him, licks his hand, rubs against him, and tries in every way that his devoted heart teaches him to attract the attention of one who is all the world to him, all my sympathies are with the dog. I watch with jealous solicitude to see if the affectionate brute gets recognition. And if by instinct, the master's hand goes to the dog's head, I am quite as glad and grateful as the recipient. If the man is absorbed and lets the animal sit patiently and adoringly watching his every expression, it seems to me I cannot refrain from calling his attention to the neglect."

The French sage Lamartine once wrote: "Whenever man is unhappy, God sends him a dog." Yet Custer, blessed with an abundance of that solace, would have none of it; his mercurial temperament, which could soar to the heights, plunged as readily to the depths.

MacTavish marched up to the porch to second Mrs. Custer's efforts in cheering the worried General by forcing his dogs on his attention. None knew better than the orderly the master's deep affection for his dogs, pets he never would sell, no matter how high a price were offered nor how numerous his pack, dogs he would sit up all night to doctor when they fell sick.

"Cardigan seems nae so well," the Scot reported. He described various symptoms of the hound's, mostly imaginary. "I dinna ken what's wrong wi' him. Maybe the General——"

Custer rose and went inside to his desk, where he always kept a book of dog remedies. A dose of medicine was concocted and poured down the throat of Cardigan, objecting reasonably but futilely. But Custer quickly relapsed into melancholy.

Mrs. Custer tried another tack. Her husband loved to have her read to him. She brought out a book and opened it on her lap.

"Listen, Autie," she insisted, "and you, too, MacTavish—
you love dogs just as much. I'm going to read you one of the
most wonderful dog stories ever written. It was written
nearly thirty-six hundred years ago on Egyptian papyrus
(that was what they called the paper they made). The only
trouble with it is, it lacks an ending. When the papyrus was
found, it was complete, but the explosion of a powder
magazine where it was carelessly stored, destroyed the last
part of the manuscript. Listen carefully because one of you
is going to have to make up an ending."

Sometimes reading, sometimes telling the tale in her own
words, Elizabeth Custer began. The charm of her beauty,
as well as the fascination of the story itself, held the two men
intent, as she told the ancient narrative of "The Doomed
Prince."

"There was once a king to whom no man-child was born,
and his heart was very sad thereat. . . ." A glimmer of
tears shone in Elizabeth's eyes. It was always a grief to her
that she and the General had had no children. Custer
reached over to pat her shoulder, and she continued.

"The king prayed for a boy from the gods of time, and
they decreed that one should be born to him. But the Hathors, the divinities to whom the King prayed for a son and
heir, at the moment of granting his plea pronounced the
doom of the unborn prince. Sternly they decreed:

" 'He shall die by the crocodile, or by the serpent, or by
the dog.'

"When the Queen bore a man-child, as the Hathors had
promised, the King strove to defend the boy against his
destiny. He built a tower of stone on a mountaintop and
kept his son there, carefully guarded, through all his child-
hood and youth. Yet when he was grown he could no longer
be kept within the narrow compass of walls. And no sooner
had he stepped into the world outside the tower than he be-

held a strange animal.

" 'What is that that runs behind a man walking on the road?' he demanded of his page.

" 'It is a dog,' the page told him.

" 'Let one be brought me exactly like it,' commanded the young prince.

"Deep was the distress of the king when he learned of his son's desire. Still he was unable to bring himself to deny it, though a dog had been named an instrument of his boy's doom.

" 'Let him be given a young running dog, lest his heart be saddened,' the King ordered.

"So upon the Prince was bestowed a coursing hound, one of those fleet animals—forerunners of our greyhounds—with which the Egyptians pursued and overtook the swiftest game. Not even when his father revealed the fate hanging over him could the Prince be persuaded to give up his pet. The dog followed faithfully at his heels when he departed from Egypt and went seeking adventure in foreign lands.

"At length he came to the court of the ruler of Naharinna whose beautiful daughter's hand was being sought by many young noblemen. The Prince became one of her suitors, concealing his identity as the heir of Pharaoh and declaring that he was a fugitive from Egypt, the son of a soldier of the chariots.

"Now the King of Naharinna shut his daughter up in a tall tower, as the Prince had been during his boyhood and youth. It was a mighty structure of seventy windows, but each and all of them were seventy cubits from the ground. And the king decreed that none should have his daughter to wife but he who could climb the sheer walls of the tower to the window where the girl waited.

"Many a vain attempt to scale the walls was made by the suitors. At length, when most of them had given up, complaining that only one who could fly like a bird could attain the lofty window, the Prince of Doom achieved the perilous ascent and entered the window to take the Princess in his arms.

"The King of Naharinna then proved false to his word. No mere fugitive from Egypt was worthy of his daughter, he avowed, and gave command that the young man be slain. But the Princess defied her father. If the young Egyptian were killed, she would die with him, she swore. So they were wedded and left the court for a dwelling.

"When the Prince's bride learned of the fate which the Hathors had decreed for her husband, she begged him earnestly: 'Slay the dog that runs before thee.'

" 'Nay,' he refused. 'I cannot slay the dog that I brought up when it was little.' "

Custer nodded violently. "Good lad, that prince!" he exclaimed.

MacTavish also broke in, thinking of Bran: "Nay, nay, he couldna!"

Mrs. Custer smiled and resumed.

"It was not the dog that first came to bring the Prince's doom upon him but the serpent. One night the Princess caught sight of a poisonous snake crawling toward the Prince to bite him as he slept. Quickly she placed a bowl of milk in its path. After greedily lapping it up, the serpent grew torpid. Then the Princess fell upon it and chopped it to bits with a hatchet." . . .

"Where's Sally Ann?" Custer demanded. "That girl would have used a derringer on that rattler or whatever it was. She ought to be hearing this yarn."

"Sally Ann has another headache," Mrs. Custer said. "Anyway, she has missed the first of the story."

"Go ahead, Libby," Custer urged.

"The valiant girl said to the husband she had saved: 'Lo,

thy god hath given one of thy dooms into thy hand.'

"Then came the crocodile. The huge creature crept up from the river one night and, seizing the Prince in its great jaws, began to drag him away. And as it crawled, the crocodile spoke to its victim:

" 'Behold, I am thy doom, following after thee.' . . .

"And there," declared Mrs. Custer, "is where the story ends."

Both Custer and MacTavish burst out in exasperation.

"That's the deuce of a place for a yarn to stop!" Custer cried in protest. "Of course you can take it for granted that the Prince or the girl did in the crocodile—"

"Ay, sir," interrupted the Scot, "but we dinna ken how it was wi' his dog. It said at the beginning that the Prince's dog might be the death of him."

"I warned you the end of the story was lost," Mrs. Custer reminded them.

"It was gunpowder destroyed the papyrus, you said, Libby?" her husband asked.

"Yes, Autie."

Custer spoke slowly and thoughtfully. "Gunpowder. It's cut off many a fine story—a man's life story—in mid-career. Sometimes just as it was rising to a glorious climax."

A sudden, deep silence fell. There was an ominously prophetic ring in the General's words. MacTavish shuffled his feet uneasily. Elizabeth Custer shuddered. Hastily she broke the silence.

"If neither of you can think of an ending, there's one a German scholar made up."

"Ah!" Custer slapped his thigh briskly. "Let's have it, Old Lady."

"The Princess came to the rescue again," Mrs. Custer related, "and killed the crocodile with her trusty hatchet.

"But those jealous suitors had never forgiven the foreigner who won the Princess from them. They banded together and came to take vengeance. Forced to flee, the young couple and their dog hid in a cave. The conspirators drew near the hiding place but might have passed it by, if the dog had not run barking to the mouth of the cave."

"Yon dog was never a staghound," MacTavish stated positively.

"The cowardly suitors dashed up and attacked in a body. Though the three in the cave made a gallant defense, they could not hold out long. The Princess, parrying a lance thrust aimed at her beloved husband's heart, received it in her own breast and died saving him. With his flashing sword the Prince cut down one foeman. His brave dog slew another with his teeth."

"Pairhaps he *was* a staghound after a'," MacTavish interjected again.

"But the odds were too heavy. Both the Prince and his dog fell. As the Prince died, he realized that his doom had been fulfilled. He had escaped the serpent and the crocodile, but the dog had unwittingly betrayed him to his enemies."

Custer, who like most people preferred a happy ending, grumbled and grew moody. His wife hastened to add:

"But the story ends happily, after all. The gods, having fulfilled the unalterable decree of fate, brought all its victims back to life because such devoted beings deserved to live."

Custer jumped to his feet. "Where's Burkman?" he shouted. "MacTavish, have him saddle up Dandy. And mounts for Mrs. Custer and Miss Lindsay, too, headache or not. It's time we took the pack out for a run. If we see any suitors, we'll sic the hounds on 'em. Failing that, we'll loose 'em on a crocodile, or at least a jackrabbit. Tallyho!"

He whistled. Yelping joyously, dogs converged on him from all sides.

Gay spirits, much more natural to General Custer, returned for a time, but they did not last long. A War Department wire curtly denied his request to remain with his regiment and ordered him to report at Washington without further delay. Reluctantly he turned over command to Major Reno, declaring he would be back as soon as possible.

There was a bare chance that Custer might return in time to lead the Seventh against the Sioux.

II

Both Peter and Lieutenant Trelford were detailed to guard duty the day Major Reno took the regiment out for a full day's march. Only the old guard and the new and various fatigue parties remained on the post.

Sternly Peter told himself: Watch yourself on this tour, Shannon. Better mind your P's and Q's and every other letter in the alphabet. Trelford's officer of the guard, and this is the first time he's had you where he wants you—right under his command. Slip up just once and that shavetail will take the greatest delight in landing on you like a ton of bricks.

Peter remembered the rattled trumpeter in the Seventh who had sounded the "General" instead of "Stables." The sarcastic Adjutant had hopped him and ordered him to blow "Recall," which corrected the mistake, and then sound the proper call. Finishing, the flustered musician tried to explain. "Sir," he said, "there must have been sand in my trumpet." Caustically the officer came back: "You need more sand in your gizzard."

Well, Lieutenant Trelford would get no chance to make any crack of that sort at the expense of Trumpeter Shannon. Every call was going to be sounded correctly and fluently and on the dot. Peter felt assured he would be ready if any call not in the day's routine were demanded—and there were more than forty in the book, not counting drill signals and inspection pieces.

There went "Assembly" for guard mount. Details for the new guard mustered from various companies, and at the guardhouse the two reliefs of the old guard off post formed up. The band marched out and took its station on the parade ground. No good outfit neglected performing this daily ceremony with precision and flourish, for it emphasized the fact that guard duty, uneventful and monotonous though it often was, nevertheless was vital.

"Adjutant's Call," and Lieutenant Cooke, sidewhiskers jutting out, and the sergeant major took their posts. The band struck up in quick time, and the details were marched out and reported. Cooke commanded: "Officers and non-commissioned officers, front and center, march." Trelford, sabre at the carry, moved forward smartly with his non-coms and was designated commander of the guard. Meticulously he inspected his men, noting every detail of uniform and giving carbines a careful going-over from bore to butt. The Lieutenant, Peter observed, never missed a trick, and his corrections of any fault were sharp and to the point.

Cooke called: "Parade rest. Sound off." The band, playing, marched down the line, countermarched, resumed its post and blared forth once more, as the guards passed in review. The intricate ceremony, its every feature exactly prescribed, concluded without a hitch, in spite of the presence of a number of recruits in the ranks.

Back at the guardhouse, Peter settled himself on a bench inside the guardroom. Cooke's and Trelford's voices drifted in through the window.

"It went off very neatly, Mr. Trelford," the Adjutant complimented.

"Yes, sir." Trelford thanked him, then chuckled. "But right in the midst of it I started thinking of that review the other day and thanking my stars guard mount is dismounted.

There was no chance for my trumpeter of the guard to get policed by his horse."

"You can't altogether blame young Shannon," Cooke protested. "That bass-drummer let go with a terrific boom right beside him."

"Right, sir," Trelford conceded. "All I hope is that no Sioux warrior ever bangs a rifle next to him."

The officers had lowered their voices, but Peter had heard all too plainly. He scowled darkly and clenched his fists.

III

Bran considered that he had been detailed to guard duty along with his master. He lay quietly at Peter's feet in the guardroom until the trumpeter rose to sound one of the routine calls. The staghound followed him out to the edge of the parade ground, took position to the trumpeter's left "at heel" and remained in an attitude of canine attention while the call was finished.

If Peter had been a sentry, Bran, unless prevented, would have walked post with him in the ancient tradition of military dogs which are as old as war itself. The armies of the Assyrians, the Persians, the Greeks, and the Romans employed them. Many a sleeping town and camp was saved by their warning barks. The dog Soter, whose alertness prevented the capture of Corinth, was pensioned for life and given a silver collar engraved, "Defender and Saviour of Corinth." In the Napoleanic wars, the dog Moustache was thrice cited; for warning of a surprise attack, for catching an Austrian spy, and for recapturing a standard from the enemy.

Now that Peter's skill in trumpeting had returned, Bran no longer uttered protesting howls. At the end of well-blown calls he wagged his tail. Peter said to himself: He has probably sensed that I'm sort of pleased with myself, and he's glad, but I'm going to take it as a compliment from a good music critic.

That night as he sounded the plaintive notes of "Taps," Peter felt certain that he would draw some complimentary tail-waggings from the dog beside him. Nor was his appreciative audience limited to one. Across the parade ground, in the lighted doorway of the Custer quarters, he saw a small figure appear and stand listening. A memory of such overwhelming poignance swept him that he could scarcely complete the call. Again he was standing on the Lindsay porch in that Texas spring night of two years ago, saying good-by to Sally Ann. "Taps," sounded by four trumpeters in harmony and with an echo, was floating to them over the Fourth's parade ground, and Sally Ann was singing its words as perhaps she was singing them now.

> *Love, good-night.*
> *Must you go*
> *When the day*
> *And the night*
> *Need you so?*
> *Though we part,*
> *Ever rest*
> *In my heart.*

Peter sounded the last, long-drawn note, and in it was all his pent-up longing. He lowered the trumpet, his throat choked. To repeat the call as he should have done was utterly beyond him. It would be some minutes before he could regain enough hold on himself to re-enter the guardroom.

The lighted doorway across the parade showed empty. That, Peter realized, was fortunate. If the appealing little figure still had been standing there, he could not have kept himself from deserting his post and running over to Sally Ann.

In the Custer kitchen, a girl was sobbing her heart out on Eliza's bosom. The soft Negro voice comforted her.

"Jes' cry yo'self out, Miss Sally Ann, and don' fret no mo'. He'll be comin' back co'tin you agin soon. He jes' cain't help hisself. Eliza knows it."

"Oh, no he won't, Eliza," the girl answered through her tears. "He's proud, and I hurt him terribly in front of everybody. Oh, why did I ever do it, Eliza?"

IV

Peter woke to insistent tugging at his sleeve. Reaching over with his other hand, he felt Bran's head. Instantly he tumbled out of his guardroom bunk—he had learned to trust the hound. Something must be wrong.

For a time, as Peter struggled awake, there was no sound save the snoring of the reliefs off post. Then clear in the night air he heard distant shouting.

"Corporal of the Guard. Post Number Eight. Fire!"

Peter ran outside, Number Eight—that was the supply train stables, and most of the mules were there. Reno had taken no wagons on his march; only a few pack animals.

The guardhouse erupted men. Peter had warmed his instrument's mouthpiece and wiped it off with the back of his hand when Lieutenant Trelford, staring toward the stables, yelled:

"Trumpeter! Where's that trumpeter?"

"Here, sir." In the darkness he was at the officer's elbow.

"Sound 'Fire Call.' "

Woe betide the frontier trumpeter who did not know "Fire Call"! The wooden buildings of a post were dreadfully vulnerable in winter when stoves were stoked red-hot against the bitter cold. Prairie grass, dried to tinder by the summer sun, was a constant menace. Always the hay and straw bedding of the stables lay ready to blaze up when a soldier or teamster sneaked a forbidden smoke—almost certainly the cause tonight.

Peter blasted out the call with all the strength of his lungs. Facing in the opposite direction, he repeated it. As he finished, he muttered under his breath: "Guess that'll keep the loot from saying anything about sand in my trumpet or lack of it in my gizzard."

Trelford, volleying orders at the non-coms of the guard, burst out: "Worst time it could happen. Not forty men left on the post. Shannon, repeat that call twice more. Then get down to those stables and see what you can do."

Windows lit up all over the post. Dark figures, running, converged on the burning stable. Already blazing embers, carried by a brisk wind, had ignited the roof of the next structure.

Cooke, Trelford, and several sergeants began organizing bucket brigades from water barrels to the fire. Peter, breathless from trumpeting, doubled after them. In the lurid glare he saw teamsters and soldiers leading mules from the burning stables. Thank God, it was the mule, not the horse stables, that were afire, even though there were few animals left in the latter! Horses became panicky with abject terror when they were caught in a burning building. Even if they broke their halter ropes, they often stayed and let themselves be burned to death. You could not lead or drive them out unless you blindfolded them. Mules were different. Did they draw their wisdom from their jackass sires? However it was, they broke free and made their escape at the first opportunity, or valiantly kicked their way through a wall, or docilely and sensibly let men rescue them.

Peter raced to one of the further, untouched stables.

Teamsters, who had led out their mules, were standing watching the fire.

"You, there," Peter shouted in a voice that rang with authority. "Harness and hitch right way. Take your wagons over there and load up empty water barrels. Fast now!"

He rode the first wagon of the string that rumbled up to the bucket brigades. Nearly all the barrels had been emptied. Sweating troopers flung them into the wagons. A grimy Trelford called out with satisfaction:

"Good going! Fill 'em up at the creek and get back here at the gallop. Hanged, if some non-com hasn't used his head!" He turned to recognize Peter directing the teamsters. "Oh," he said, "it's you."

Over the half-mile to the creek the wagons roared, mule teams at a dead gallop, teamsters yelling and cracking whips, barrels rattling in the beds like giant castanets. Precious water replenished, the wagons came clattering and careening back. They were too late to save the first stable, but the fire in the second was controlled. Trip after trip the wagons made, and troopers drenched other smouldering roofs.

Further along the line a gust carried a spark to still another stable. Tongues of flames soared up. A teamster shouted that all the mules were out of it, and fire fighters, still hard pressed elsewhere, were compelled to let it burn.

Again Peter felt a tug at his sleeve. It was Bran, who seldom had left his side. The dog all but told him words: "Quick! We're needed at that stable."

Peter tried to disregard the summons. Somehow he found it beyond his power. Drawn by Bran's insistence, he followed the staghound at the double. As they approached, Peter heard a racket which proved the teamster had been mistaken. There was at least one mule still in there. The night resounded to angry braying and a thunderous rat-tat-tat of iron-shod heels on boards.

Ah, Stable B. That would be Old Pizen.

Thick smoke belched out of the door in crimsoned billows. Hoofbeats rang out louder but there was no splintering crash in answer. Even Old Pizen could not batter himself an exit.

Peter hesitated at the door. What was an old mule's life to his? The beast, as he nearly had before, probably would kick his would-be rescuer to death.

The trumpeter jammed his hat down on his head and drew a long breath. He and the dog plunged into the flaming stable.

Choking, blinded, he groped his way forward. Bran rubbed against him. Peter grasped his collar and the staghound led him on. Yonder a bale of hay blazed up to show Old Pizen, still tethered by the double-strength halter rope used on him. At once the redoubtable old rascal stopped kicking. Peter untied him without difficulty and rushed him out of the stable.

Outside, Peter beat out the sparks in Bran's hide and his own uniform. He reached up to pat Old Pizen's neck and said:

"That ought to show you, you old battering-ram, that I've got no hard feelings."

V

The next morning, skin blistered, eyebrows scorched, Peter reported to the Adjutant, as ordered.

"Fine work last night, Shannon," Lieutenant Cooke complimented, stroking one luxuriant sideburn.

"Thank you, sir."

"Want to show you a paragraph in a regimental order. Major Reno or the General will sign it—whoever returns first."

Peter's eyes quickly caught his name under a promotions heading:

"To be Corporal-Trumpeter: Trumpeter Peter Shannon, Hq. Co."

As he spoke his thanks and saluted, he heard the Adjutant remark:

"Lieutenant Trelford's recommendation."

The first rung of the ladder! But Peter, striding back to barracks, found his elation somewhat tempered. If only the promotion had not come through Trelford. It was a lot easier to have a rival who treated you like dirt and made mean cracks about your misfortunes. A decent fellow who saw you got a boost if you deserved one—that made it tough.

13: REUNION AT FORT ABE

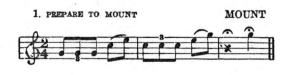

I

OVER the "whispering wires," as the Indians called the tele-
graph, bad news had reached Fort Abraham Lincoln. The
officers' mess and the barracks of the Seventh buzzed with it.

General Crook's column had suffered a severe repulse at
the hands of the Sioux and Cheyennes. Marching north in
bitter, unseasonable cold, Crook had sent three squadrons
of cavalry ahead for a surprise attack on the big village of
Chief Two Moons, beside the bluffs of the Powder River.
A brave Indian herdboy, though covered by an officer's revolver, whooped an alarm, and the charging cavalrymen met
a storm of withering fire. Horses plunged, reared and

crashed down, but ranks, closing up, galloped on to capture the village and Indian pony herd.

As the cavalry set fire to the lodges, the hostiles counter-attacked. Troopers fought them off through a morning so frigid that ears, noses, feet and hands froze. Burning lodges gave a little warmth, but some soldiers were forced to the drastic resort of plunging congealing hands through air-holes into the ice-locked river. Nevertheless, the defense held, and Crook could be counted on to come up soon in support.

But the colonel commanding the squadrons in action failed to hold his ground. Suddenly and inexplicably, he ordered a retreat. So hasty was the retirement, one wounded trooper was shamefully abandoned to torture. Triumphant warriors in hot pursuit recaptured many of their ponies. When the squadrons returned to the main force, the furious Crook relieved the commander, who was court-martialed and resigned, his career wrecked.

The news of defeat caused grim looks in the Seventh, yet they were not long in lightening, for that defeat was on another outfit's record. "Now if the Seventh had been there," the men of that mettlesome regiment told each other, "it wouldn't have happened." And it was clear to everyone that Crook's repulse, by delaying the entire campaign, would allow more time for Custer to return, resume command and lead his own regiment against the Sioux.

But would Old Curley make the grade? Here, too, the news was gloomy. Custer was in hot water up to his neck. The Seventh heard that his testimony had deeply offended Grant—that some of it had been branded hearsay, not evidence—that the President had kept him sitting in Washington, refusing either to see him or to let him leave—that Generals Sherman, Sheridan, and Terry, especially the last-mentioned, who was conducting the campaign and were begging for Custer's services, had vainly interceded.

At last came the break. Grant had yielded. The Seventh's commanding officer was on his way back to his regiment. "Custer's luck."

The Seventh began preparing a celebration for its returning leader. No formal review, with the regiment parading in his honor, would serve. Only something unusual, hilarious and uproarious would suit the high spirits of the jubilant General.

Some genius suggested a mule race, with officers, General Custer included, as jockeys.

II

Peter Shannon, told by MacTavish that Mrs. Custer wished to see him, obeyed with reluctance. It was likely to be some ruse to bring him and Sally Ann together; older women simply could not resist matchmaking. Of course, it was all well-meant but none of her business. Peter was glad now he had resisted his impulse to run over to Sally Ann that night when he sounded "Taps." Better, far better let it end—as it had ended—as a boy-and-girl love affair. How could it ever come to anything more? When Lieutenant Trelford, plainly a rising young officer, inevitably won the girl, there would be far less bitterness in store for a disinterested party than for a defeated rival.

Peter made his decision. If Sally Ann appeared, he would treat her with cold formality.

But Mrs. Custer was alone on the porch when Peter walked up. He lifted his forage cap and whether his summons was a subterfuge or not, immediately melted, as all men did when confronted by Elizabeth Custer's charm. At once she greeted him:

"Congratulations, Corporal Shannon. I'm told you did marvelous things at the fire. Your stripes are well deserved, and may you change them for a sergeant's before long!"

"Thanks a lot, Mrs. Custer." Peter glowed with pleasure.

"I'm going to ask a favor of you, Corporal."

"I'll be glad to do anything I can," Peter blurted, then bit his lip. This would be some trick to reconcile him and Sally Ann.

But he was entirely mistaken, for Mrs. Custer asked: "You've heard about the mule race?"

"Yes, ma'am, a bit."

"I'm so happy it's to be that and not a horse race. I hate horse races that people bet on, and when our officers ride their chargers in steeplechases, it's dreadfully dangerous. For the mule race, there'll just be a prize, and the slowest mule—the one that comes in last—will be the winner. Nobody will be hurt if he's tossed off that way, and it's all going to be so funny. Now General Custer is going to ride, but he'll be back too late to choose and train his mount. If he were here, of course he'd pick the most stubborn mule in the regiment."

"Yes, ma'am. Old Pizen."

Eliza called from the door. "That's the mos' contrary animule ever I see."

"Old Pizen it is." Mrs. Custer's laughter was silvery. "Would you mind training him for the General?"

"I'd be glad to try. Old Pizen's my friend now, I think."

"He ought to be, after you kept him from being burned to a crisp. Thank you ever so much, Corporal. It'll be such fun! Good-by."

Peter, leaving, was conscious of aching disappointment. There had been no sign whatever of Sally Ann. She was probably out riding with Trelford.

III

Down at the mule stables, officer-jockeys were selecting their mounts. Each merrily made it a point to pick the most obstreperous animal available. Teamsters pushed forward, enthusiastically recommending some member of their own teams.

"Here you are, sir. If it's laziness and a slow freight the captain's looking for, this here brute takes the cake." . . . "Take Prairie Rose here, sir. She ain't never been ridden and she'll be better'n a balloon." . . . "Lootenant, if you want to come in last, Rattler's yer mule. When he ain't a-kicking, he's a-backing up."

It shortly became apparent to Peter that he had his work cut out for him as Old Pizen's trainer. Jake Small, the mule's teamster, washed his hands of the affair.

"All right, Shannon," he said. "Be a danged fool if yuh want. I've druv that mule years and I know better. Reckon you don't. First he kicks your slats in when you jined up. Next you gits yerself singed savin' him when the consarned old critter is 'bout to git burned up like he deserves. Now what you fixin' to do? Git the Gin'ral up on his back. Man, there's stuff in the Articles of War agin that. Malishous an' murderous assault on a superior officer—that's what. Come sunrise after that there race, you and Old Pizen'll be facin' a firing squad together."

Peter laughed and answered: "Not on your life. I'm acting under orders."

The volunteer trainer began operations. Manifestly Pizen was grateful toward him, but any endeavor to make a riding animal out of the beast was asking too much. After several near-catastrophes, Peter devised and, with the help of a saddler, made a special harness. Huge blinders were strapped over the mule's head so that he was virtually masked. A complicated network of leather straps bound him fore and aft. Only then was Peter able to vault into the saddle and maneuver the mule about to a limited extent.

As busy as the trainers was the racing committee, who spared nothing by way of fanfares and flourishes on the forthcoming mule derby. A program, featuring the distinguished ancestry of the entries, was drawn up and sent to the printer in Bismarck.

U.S. ARMY COURSE
Fort Abraham Lincoln
GREAT MULE RACE
One mile—or Any Fraction

1. General Custer enters Old Pizen, by Strychnine, out of Ground Glass; second dam, Hemlock, by Venomous, out of Prussic Acid. Age, older than Methuselah. Colors, scared pink.

2. Colonel Tom Custer enters Hard Tack, by Commissary, out of Weevils; second dam, Polly Tix, by Gravy, out of Pocket. Age, old enough to know better. Colors, seasick green.

3. Captain Yates enters Carbine, by Breech Loader, out of Magazine; second dam, Misfire, by Kick-Back, out of Luck. Age, sweet sixteen. Colors, black and blue.

4. Lieutenant Moylan enters Break-Neck, by Runaway, out of Wouldn't Go; second dam, Bruises, by Contusion, out of Collision. Age, hoary. Colors, dipped.

5. Lieutenant Trelford enters Lethargic, by Tardy, out of A.W.O.L.; second dam, (not worth one). Age, (she's a lady and won't tell). Colors: ashen white. . . .

So it ran through thirteen entries. More advance publicity was provided by industriously-spread rumors which were printed in the paper. One item read:

ONE "SHERIDAN'S RIDE" ENOUGH

With feelings of deep regret we announce that Major General Phil Sheridan, commanding the Department of the West, will not ride in the Great Mule Race at Fort Abe Lincoln. This may be relied upon as positive. The General has paid his forfeit. He had bought him a little bob-tailed, blue, mouse-colored mule, and was training him like Sam Hill, when an idea struck him: to wit, that there were poets in Dakota Territory. Suppose, he thought with dismay, one of those fellows got off a poem entitled: "Sheridan's Mule Ride"! The dread possibility was more than he could contemplate, and, as aforesaid, he paid his forfeit. Thomas Buchanan Read's poem, "Sheridan's Ride," came near ruining him, the General says. Ever since that, people have been *riding* him. Thus we have it on the best authority that the Great Mule Race will be run "with Sheridan twenty miles away"—at least.

In the band barracks, a chorus of soldiers practiced every night with musical accompaniment, to be ready to sound off before the race with a highly appropriate ditty: *Whoa, Mule, Whoa!*

IV

The day of the mule race, as the reporter for the Bismarck paper put it, dawned bright and clear. He also noted that a heavy rain the night before had raised the odds on good mud-mules by making the track heavy and—fortunately for the riders—softer.

Custer's return the night before had drawn no heartier cheers than his appearance today, clad in a ridiculous parody of racing silks. All the other officer-jockeys also had shed their dignity for comical costumes. Troopers, solidly lining the course, yelled with delight and, free of the restraints of discipline, shouted jocular comments. The racket rose to a crescendo as trainers led up the indignant mounts, headed by Peter and Old Pizen, whose safety-first accoutrements gave him the look of some fantastic beast that nobody could expect to see except after eating five welsh rarebits and being afflicted with a very bad dream.

The glee club, seconded by the band, burst into *Whoa, Mule, Whoa!*

> *I went to see Miss Liza Jane,*
> *To take her for a ride.*
> *My ol' mule was so frisky,*
> *He'd run awhile, then slide.*

> ### Chorus

> *Whoa, mule, whoa!*
> *Whoa, mule, I say!*
> *Just hop right in, Miss Liza,*
> *And hold on to the sleigh.*

> *We went down through old Tucker's lane,*
> *The neighbors they did stare.*
> *I wanted to kiss Liza,*
> *But I couldn't do it there.*

> ### Chorus

> *Whoa, mule, whoa!*
> *You could hear them holler:*
> *"Better tie a knot in that mule's tail,*
> *Or he'll jump right through the collar."*

> *I took Miss Liza to the parson's,*
> *Miss Liza, you keep cool.*
> *I sho' would like to kiss you,*
> *But I'se busy with this mule.*

Chorus

Whoa, mule, whoa!
Whoa, mule, I say!
If you get out, Miss Liza Jane,
It'll be our weddin' day.

When applause for the singers had died down, General Custer motioned the other riders to gather around him.

"Gentlemen," he announced, "you have all doubtless been training your mounts to the best of your ability, in spite of the fact that you knew the winner would be the mule that came in last. As gentlemen riders, you will try to stay aboard and urge your steeds to their utmost speed, lose or not. But that is too much to ask. So the racing committee has established a new rule, in the name of justice, equity, and jollity. Each rider will now step up to the Adjutant and draw lots. Everybody'll draw some other mule than his own to ride. Each jockey will thus prove his superb mulemanship on an unfamiliar mount and do his best to bring the other fellow's mule in first and lose for him."

Shouts of delight echoed across the parade ground. They rose to a climax when Trelford drew Old Pizen.

The Lieutenant grinned as he said: "Something tells me the General didn't want to ride this old devil."

Custer grinned back. "On the contrary, I was looking forward to it, but I thought he wouldn't give me much sport with all this harness on him. Corporal Shannon, take off all those trappings. Mr. Trelford, I want you to have a real ride and bring him in first, even if it makes me lose. Pizen's practically blinded and hamstrung the way he is."

Amid howls of acclaim and protest, Peter dared step forward and speak earnestly. "I beg the General's pardon, but honestly, sir, that harness ought to stay on. Nobody can ride Pizen without it. He knows me but he wouldn't let even me on his back unharnessed."

Custer shouted with laughter, but Trelford bent a caustic look on Peter. "Get all that truck off that mule, Shannon," he ordered.

Peter was certain that Trelford's look said as plainly as if he had spoken, "It doesn't prove a thing that you couldn't ride him unharnessed." The trumpeter flushed brick-red and clamped his lips shut.

He sternly reminded himself: That's what an enlisted man gets for speaking out of turn. You've been in the Army long enough to know the motto of the man in the ranks: Keep your trap closed and never volunteer for anything. Forget that just once and you wish you hadn't.

Roughly he stripped off the mule's protective harness. Old Pizen, blinders off, blinked, turned his head and regarded his trainer as if to say: I only wore that stuff to please you. Glad to get it off. Much obliged.

Jockeys stood to mule. The starter's pistol cracked, and every officer vaulted on to the back of his mount. Indignant squeals and outraged braying filled the air. Mules dashed off in every direction except down the track. For Mrs. Custer, gripping the rail of the ladies' stand, the spectacle merged into a mêlée of flying hoofs, wildly switching shaved tails, splotches of fantastic racing silks, spurring legs, and whacking whips. That good lady would have been distressed to learn that the troopers along the course were enthusiastically betting on the race, wagering up to a month's pay. They yelled themselves hoarse for their favorites.

"Go it, Old Curley! . . . Hooray for Yates! . . . Ride him, cowboy. . . . Kick him in the slats, Loot. You ain't half tryin'!"

It was the rank and file's day to howl without hindrance. Only once was any restraint clamped on. When an embittered soldier with a grudge against an officer yelped, "Hope that mule kills you, you skunk!" a big first sergeant clamped a heavy hand on his shoulder and growled: "That's enough o' that, bucko."

Custer, Yates, and several others had mastered their mounts and were galloping for the finish. Here and there silks flashed in the sun, as jockeys were bucked off. Some remounted, others hotly pursued their vagrant steeds. But most eyes were fixed on Old Pizen. Trelford had got aboard and miraculously was still there. Old Pizen stood stock-still on the starting line, ears aslant, an expression of utter and side-splitting amazement on his long face.

Trelford began to ply whip and spurs. Then Old Pizen came out of his trance. He shot into the air like a jumping-jack and hit the ground kicking. He revolved like a whirligig. He bucked like an outlaw broncho. His jockey gave a pretty exhibition of riding but only for a few seconds. Then he was pitched so high into the air that he was half-stunned by his fall. Dazed, he began slowly picking himself up.

Old Pizen was by no means satisfied. He had been mortally insulted. A backward glance showed him an ideal target— his jockey on hands and knees. The mule took aim and cocked his mighty haunches for a lethal kick that would have crippled his enemy for life.

Peter was close enough for a plunging rush. His shoulder struck the mule on the flank. Barely deflected, the iron-shod heels whistled past their intended victim. Then Peter caught the angry animal by the bridle, soothing him. Jake Small and three troopers came to his aid.

Old Pizen's determined attempt at assault and battery had stolen the show. Spectators abandoned the race and converged on the focus of excitement from all quarters. Few noticed that Captain Yates' mule, Lieutenant McIntosh clinging ingloriously to his neck, had buck-jumped across the finish line last, winning the race.

The crowd watched the dazed Trelford stagger to his feet. He stood swaying for a minute or so while his head cleared. Comrades gathered around to see if he were hurt. He grinned slowly and denied it. Some pointed to Corporal Shannon, telling the Lieutenant what had happened. Trelford thrust through the group and unhesitatingly strode straight over to Peter.

"Corporal, I owe you an apology," he acknowledged, "and a lot more than that. If you hadn't shoved that mule off center, I'd have spent the next campaign in a hospital cot—or a pine box. I'll always be grateful. Will you shake my hand?"

Debonair despite his bedraggled silks, the Lieutenant offered his hand.

"Yes, sir," said Peter and exchanged handclasps. But his eyes and his voice were cold. True, this was a handsome apology. "Handsome is as handsome does." *Noblesse oblige.* Yet it is not easy to accept amends from a man whose contempt you have sensed nor from a rival. Peter could not help noticing that Sally Ann had run up with the rest to find out if her best beau had been hurt by his tumble.

Deliberately Peter turned his back and led Old Pizen off to the stable.

v

Down at the corrals, a consignment of remounts for the Seventh had arrived. They were strong, sturdy horses, averaging about four years old, and, once they were conditioned, they would stand the long marches of the hard campaign to come, though many of them could not match the speed of the lighter Indian ponies. They were being assigned to various companies according to their color.

Several officers who needed chargers had hurried down.

Old Pizen shot into the air like a jumping-jack and hit the ground kicking. He revolved like a whirligig. He bucked like an outlaw broncho

They were privileged to buy a horse from the Government at cost price, which amounted to about $100. It was thus Custer and Keogh had acquired their excellent mounts, Dandy and Comanche.

As one man, the officers made a beeline for a good-looking black gelding with a white blaze and four white stockings. The black was each one's first choice. A hot argument had resulted in an agreement to decide the matter by tossing a coin when Burkman, Custer's horse orderly, hurried up and haltered the animal.

"This here one ain't in the market," Burkman gruffly declared.

"See here," a captain objected, "the General already has a fine string and I—"

"The black's private-owned, sir," Burkman announced with finality and led him off for grooming, followed by jealous glances.

Once more Corporal Shannon received a summons to the Custer quarters. "Friend of yours from the 4th Cavalry, they sez," the messenger imparted.

Major Lindsay perhaps. Of course Peter could not avoid paying his respects, although he did not care to return to the Fourth now. The Major probably had come up to escort his daughter Sally Ann back to their station.

No one was visible in front of the Custers' house as Peter arrived. But around the corner came a girl in a riding habit, leading a black horse, saddled and bridled, a black horse who tossed his fine head and stepped out proudly on his four white-stockinged feet.

Sally Ann and the horse suddenly halted. The black's small, well-shaped ears pricked forward as he caught sight of the approaching soldier. He neighed long and joyously. Sally Ann loosed him.

Justin, the black Morgan, trotted straight to his old master. Peter's arms went around his neck and he buried his face in the glossy mane.

Behind him a soft voice, trembling and a little uncertain, was saying:

"Peter dear, I couldn't help it. I had to send for Justin. I knew there wasn't any other way I could get you to speak to me again."

Time rolled back. The same scene had been played three years ago in Texas, with a boy and a girl facing each other beside this horse. Hands caressing a velvety, gently-snorting muzzle met and clung. Ardent gray eyes lost themselves in shining brown ones.

A scurry, and a big dog thrust into the group. Bran and Justin rubbed noses, sniffing by way of introduction, while Peter and Sally Ann stood there, wordlessly happy.

"As striking a tableau as I've ever seen!"

It was Lieutenant Trelford's voice. No one had heard him stroll up.

"Hello, Miss Sally Ann. How are you, Corporal?" the intruder greeted. "Say, whose horse is that? A grand Morgan. I tried to buy him down at the corral but Burkman said——"

"He's Miss Lindsay's, sir."

"No," Sally Ann contradicted. "He's P——. I mean, he's Corporal Shannon's."

"As a private mount, he couldn't be, could he?" Trelford questioned.

"She means I used to ride him in the Fourth, sir."

"But," Sally Ann began helplessly, "but I was going to give——"

"Oh." Trelford looked puzzled, then deeply thoughtful. "I see. You both used to ride this Morgan in the Fourth. Well, anyway, Shannon couldn't ride him now. The General mounts all his musicians on grays."

"But he must ride him. Peter, please, for my sake. Get on him. Can't you see Justin is longing for you to take him for a gallop."

Peter could not resist the beseeching brown eyes. He swung into the saddle. How good it was to be on his beloved horse's back again. Justin snorted with pleasure and stamped a white forefoot.

"Go ahead, Corporal," Trelford urged. "You're off duty. As a matter of fact, I was just about to invite Miss Sally Ann riding. Here's my orderly with the horses. I picked out the little sorrel for you, Sally Ann. You'll like him."

Peter saluted and rode off. Sitting Justin back of the stables, he watched Sally Ann and Trelford riding off across the prairie. The sorrel kept pushing up close to the officer's mount. Repeatedly Sally Ann reined the animal away to a proper distance. The sorrel persistently closed in again until the girl and the man were riding knee to knee like a pair of lovers.

"Hang that fellow!" Peter muttered between set teeth. "I see why he picked out that horse for Sally Ann. That blamed sorrel's a 'snuggler.' "

14: BUFFALO HUNT

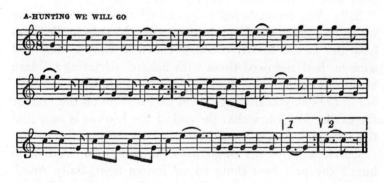

A-HUNTING WE WILL GO

I

"OIL up your shooting-irons and buckle on your spurs, Calamity Jane the Second. You're going to get a crack at some big game. We're off on a buffalo hunt."

Custer beamed down on Sally Ann, as he spoke. "You might call this hunt the opening of the campaign for the Seventh," he went on. "We're going under orders. A sizable herd's been reported drifting toward the territory where the hostiles off the reservation are gathering. I'm to drive it south, away from the Indians. They'd be mighty glad to get their hands on that meat."

The hunt was good strategy, as the General had indicated, for the very livelihood of the tribes—their food, clothing, and shelter—was the buffalo. The fates of the two, the red man and the bison, were inseparably joined. Under the onslaughts of hunters, vast herds had dwindled with appalling swiftness. In 1866, General Sheridan had estimated that there were 100 million buffalo on the mid-western plains. Now, ten years later, the animal was nearing extinction. Last year Sheridan had persuaded the Texas Legislature not to enact game laws protecting the buffalo, conceding that the hide hunters, by destroying the Indians' commissary, were contributing more toward his conquest than the Army had been able to achieve in thirty years.

Sally Ann remembered a legend of the Kiowas, a tribe which had given the Fourth many a hard battle in Texas— how the Great Spirit, creating the first Kiowa man and woman, had endowed them with a herd, declaring: "Here are the Buffalo. They shall be your food and your raiment, but in the day you shall see them perish from off the face of the earth, then know that the end of the Kiowas is near and the Sun set."

Custer slapped his thigh with his gauntlets. "A buffalo hunt's the next best thing to an Indian fight, Sally Ann," he declared exuberantly. "We're in luck to get this hunt in before the regiment goes after the Sioux. That'll be any day now, with the weather warming up the way it is."

"You promise I can go on the hunt, General?" the girl asked eagerly.

In the 4th Cavalry, Sally Ann had ridden to the hounds on regimental hunts, when the quarry was no fox but a coyote, but she never had hunted buffalo. The Fourth's commander, General Mackenzie, a bachelor, disapproved of women participating in so dangerous a sport. Riders in hot pursuit were liable to a bad fall if their mounts stepped in a prairie dog hole. The furious charges of a wounded bison were plenty for a man on an agile horse to handle. To face dismounted the rushes of those huge humped beasts was more than the most experienced hunter lightly risked. Only fast, straight shooting could save a man then.

But it was the custom in the Seventh to invite its ladies to the hunts. Mrs. Custer could not resist the exciting spectacle nor the opportunity to watch, shaking like a leaf, the bold exploits of her General. Two daring sisters, the wives of Lieutenants McIntosh and Gibson, galloped and blazed away with the field.

"You're really going to let me go?" Sally Ann begged again.

Custer gazed fondly at her flushed, pretty face. "You bet I am, my dear. Why, without you it wouldn't be half as exciting."

The General spoke more truly than he realized.

II

Uniform for the hunt was go-as-you-please. Custer wore his famous fringed buckskin. Other officers followed his example or donned corduroy jackets over gaudy shirts, bought from the sutler. The two companies detailed for escort made themselves comfortable in nondescript clothing, though the prevailing hue was Army blue. However, loaded carbines and revolvers lent a look of military readiness.

Sally Ann found a moment for a few words with Peter, as he trotted up on Humpty, leading her mount Justin.

"I do wish you'd ride Justin instead of me, Pete," she

pleaded.

Peter frowned. "And let you ride that sorrel?"

The girl laughed. "I should say not! You know that rascal, Phil Trelford, spent days training that horse to be a 'snuggler.'"

"So I noticed."

"Oh, did you? Well, I bet you didn't see me fix him later. Phil was riding on my near side, of course, so the sorrel could snuggle me right up to him. I just couldn't keep my horse away. So when Phil wasn't expecting anything, I gave his horse a sharp kick in the belly."

Sally Ann giggled merrily. "His mount jumped like a jackrabbit and started to run away. I thought Phil was going off."

Peter laughed in relief. "Good for you, Sally Ann. Be sure *you* don't get thrown in this hunt."

"I'll sit tight, Pete."

She gathered Justin's reins in her right hand and grasped the second pommel of the side-saddle. Peter cupped his hands, and the girl placed her left foot in them. Demurely she arranged her habit's wide-flowing skirt, weighted down with tiny bags of shot sewn in the hem. Then she rested her left hand on Peter's shoulder and as he lifted, she sprang up and seated herself sideways on the saddle, hooking a knee over the horn.

"My stars and upsadaisy!" she exclaimed. "What a way for an able-bodied gal to have to get on a horse! Wish I were a brat again and could climb aboard all by myself and ride astride like a man and not have to be ladylike. But since I had to be hoisted"—Sally Ann bent her head, crowned with a huntsman's cap fitting close over her chestnut curls, and flashed Peter a glance from her brown eyes—"well, I can't think of anybody I'd rather have do it. Thank you, sir."

Heart pounding, Peter turned to mount Humpty. He enjoyed noting Lieutenant Trelford hurrying up, obviously disappointed that he had arrived too late to help Sally Ann mount.

Now all the hunting party was in the saddle. The band rode up to take its place in the column, and the wagons, laden with mess chests, provisions, forage, and tenting, rolled up in the rear.

"*Garryowen* leads the hunt!" Custer cried and signaled the band, "Sound off." To the regimental tune, the cavalcade moved out. Maida, Bran, and the other staghounds, foxhounds, and greyhounds trotted along at the flanks, joyfully cavorting.

Miles lay behind them when the party halted for a picnic lunch. The march was resumed after a short rest. In midafternoon, the distant scouts were seen circling their horses. Buffalo had been sighted. Custer shifted from Vic to Dandy, and the other officers also changed to the buffalo horses they had been sparing by having their orderlies lead them.

The two Custer brothers sounded flourishes on their hunting horns, seconded by blasts by every trumpeter present. Whooping, Custer shot away at a gallop, officers and troopers stringing out behind. The ladies drew opera glasses from little velvet bags and leveled them. Yonder, like a vast stream of brown lava, the herd flowed over the prairie, submerging clumps of sagebrush. Under the threat of onrushing horsemen and dogs, the stream slowed and halted, the great beasts lifting their heads to gaze curiously and stupidly at approaching death. Then the stream turned suddenly into a rushing torrent. Switching little tufted tails, bulls, cows, and bawling calves fled in panic. The prairie shook to the thunder of pounding hoofs. Rising dust clouds were pierced by spurts of red flame, followed seconds later by the crackle of gunfire. Back in the ambulance, the surgeon expectantly laid out bandages and opened his instrument case. It was a rare buffalo hunt that produced no casualties. Swiftly the dust clouds rolled further into the distance.

"I can't see a thing," Sally Ann cried. "Come on." She gave Justin his head. With the sisters beside her, she galloped after the hunt.

Mrs. Custer hurriedly beckoned to Peter. "Corporal," she called, "ride after that reckless girl and watch out for her. She might have an accident and I can't—"

Peter wheeled his mount and was off. Slow old Humpty rocked along far in rear of the racing horsewomen.

Amid the dust and tumult, flashes of vivid action rewarded the venturesome Sally Ann. She saw eager officers pick out quarries and ride down on them, reins loose on chargers' necks, rifles blazing. Divided into two teams, they hunted in hot rivalry, for, according to custom, the team making the most kills would drink the other's wine at mess that evening. Each successful nimrod dismounted to cut out the tongue of the buffalo he brought down, hanging the trophy at his saddle, both to mark his score and add to the feast. The regiment would regale itself for days on this delicious meat and tender steaks cut from the humps of young bulls— welcome change from stringy beef and salt pork.

Nor was there less sport for the troopers than the officers, despite the former's slower horses, since there was plenty of game for all. Carbines blazed away, and brown heaps began to dot the prairie. Yet the buffalo fought back. Sally Ann saw one trooper and his horse butted into a creek by an enraged bull. A second horse was gored but managed to plunge clear with his rider. Yonder a novice shot himself through the sleeve with his own pistol, as his mount dodged a bull's charge. A sergeant was thrown and knocked unconscious. Picked up by the ambulance, the victim revived as the surgeon was examining him.

"Humph," remarked the sawbones in disappointed tones. "All you've got is a broken arm. Thought I was going to have a real job to do on you."

The three Army women, galloping over a divide, found themselves riding to the hounds. Here the pack was enjoying a buffalo hunt of its own. Above the clamor rang the bell-like bay of the foxhounds. The fleet greyhounds easily passed and turned buffalo which were faster than an ordinary horse on level ground. But it was the big staghounds that were the real kings of the chase. Except for elk, counterpart of the stags their ancestors had pursued in the Highlands, the bison was the favorite quarry of the staghounds. By twos and threes they closed in on a beast they had marked down. Juno sprang straight at the nose of one buffalo, while Maida seized him by an ear and Lufra attacked his flank. But others of the pack found the quarry too much for them. One buffalo lowered his shaggy head, caught an unwary dog and tossed him thirty feet in the air. The yelping animal hit the ground running and fled with his tail between his legs. While some of the dogs were persuaded that discretion was the better part of valor and contented themselves with yapping at a safe distance, the rest rushed back into the fray all the more savagely.

Sally Ann and her friends hallooed shrilly, as Bran, Tuck, and Blucher cut out the triumphant buffalo, the largest bull in the herd, and drove him toward a solitary horseman galloping up out of the dust.

The lone hunter was General Custer. Dashing up, he motioned the women back, called off the hounds and drove Dandy at the big fellow. The bull thundered off at astonishing speed, Custer hot after him.

This chase was beyond Sally Ann's powers of resistance. She spoke to Justin and gave him his head. The black Morgan spurted forward at a pace that soon left the sisters far behind. Racing along on a parallel course with hunter and hunted, Sally witnessed a remarkable exhibition by horse and horseman.

Dandy darted after the buffalo like an arrow sped from a bow. He swerved to avoid a large patch of sagebrush, then suddenly leaped a solitary clump that barred his path. Another rider might have been unseated but not Custer—he sat his saddle in perfect harmony with every motion. The horse began to overtake the lumbering but speedy beast. Now the intelligent Dandy closed in on the prey's flank. As well as Custer he knew the bison's vulnerable point— knew that he must bring his master into position to place his bullets just behind the fore-shoulder.

Sally Ann, racing along at a dead gallop, marveled that the General need give his fine steed no guidance whatever but let the reins lie loose on his neck. Custer apparently had emptied his rifle earlier in the hunt, for he left it in its boot and drew both revolvers from their holsters. Now Dandy drew nearly abreast—crowded in so close he almost rubbed the buffalo's side. But before Custer could fire, the beast whirled abruptly toward his pursuers.

A scream of warning choked in Sally Ann's throat. Nothing, she was certain, could save Dandy from impalement on those short, wicked horns, with Custer going down to have his life stamped out by the sharp hoofs.

She had underestimated the best buffalo horse in the regiment. Dandy plunged away at an abrupt tangent. Hardly had the horns raked past him with scant clearance than he closed in again. Custer, yelling, emptied his Colts, one after another, into the massive brown body.

Sally Ann found herself yelling, too. She saw the big animal stagger and slow down. A hundred yards further and he was reeling. On the edge of a broad wallow he plowed to a stop. Bellowing, he toppled over the rim, fell in with a crash and lay still.

Custer greeted Sally Ann with a victorious shout as she galloped up.

"Good girl! You sure did stick with me. Look at this fellow! Bet he weighs a ton and a half."

The two rode down into the wallow and dismounted to inspect the fallen animal closely. Custer could not have greatly exaggerated its weight. They walked around and around the bull, admiringly examining it.

"Say, we've got to have a photograph of this," the General cried. "I'm going to get Yates to bring the camera. You stay here, Sally Ann, and don't let anybody else claim this fellow. You'll be all right with that horse of yours, and here, take my rifle." He reloaded the magazine of his repeater. "Be right back." Custer flung himself on Dandy and was gone.

Sally Ann had stifled a protest. She scanned the huge body beside her and shuddered a little. Quickly she led Justin up out of wallow and moved a good space away. Suddenly she was desperately lonely. The noise of the hunt grew faint, as the herd was driven southward. There was no sign of Mrs. Gibson and Mrs. McIntosh. Far outdistanced, perhaps they had lost her in the dust or come up during the minutes she and Custer were down in the wallow and hidden from view. Then, seeing no one, they probably had galloped off in another direction.

Under the girl's searching eyes the prairie stretched out emptily. Sally Ann trembled a little again.

She set her jaw. "Where's your nerve?" she scolded herself. "You're acting like a tenderfoot—like some girl who has just graduated from Miss Smithson's Finishing School for Young Ladies and come West. Come out of it!"

With a touch of bravado she turned Justin loose to graze. No need to hobble or hold him. He would come to her promptly when she whistled.

Fatigue suddenly flooded over her. She sat down on the grass, settling her skirt around her, and waited.

III

After the clamor of the hunt, there was something disquieting about the present stillness. To break it Sally Ann began to hum *Buffalo Girls,* only to stop it after a bar or two; somehow it seemed less appropriate than it should. There was no sign of Custer nor anyone else yet. Yonder Justin grazed peacefully, steadily wandering farther and farther away to greener grass.

Sally Ann saw the horse's head come up at the moment her own ears caught a strange sound. She stared rapidly around her but could not locate its origin. It sounded like deep, inhuman groaning, with puffing and scuffling. The girl jumped to her feet in alarm. Still she could see nothing.

The noise grew louder. Something was coming out of the broad wallow there. Sally Ann saw a crest of matted brown mane rise slowly over the rim. A moment more and round red eyes, glaring malignantly, were fixed on her. Stentorian snorts issued through distended nostrils from which crimson trickles dribbled. Custer's bullets had stunned the big bull and inflicted mortal wounds, but a last upsurge of life had revived him. Now the final remnant of his mighty strength was driving him with fierce urgency to take revenge before he died.

Sally Ann stood frozen with terror while the bull, grunting and gasping, dragged himself up out of the wallow. Flanks heaving, swaying on his feet, he stayed rooted for merciful seconds after he had regained the level of the prairie. Though he was twenty yards away, the monster loomed over the girl, huge and horrible, like an overhanging mass of earth on the verge of an avalanche.

Sally Ann wrenched herself out of her panicky trance. With swift motions she scooped up Custer's rifle and levered a cartridge into the chamber.

Still the great buffalo stood there, gathering himself. Sally Ann whistled shrilly for Justin, not daring altogether to take her gaze from the bison. Out of the corners of her eyes she noted how the black Morgan stood shaking, not daring to obey her signal. With sinking heart she realized that for any horse to approach riderless in the face of an enraged buffalo about to charge was more than anyone could expect. She steeled herself and looked away.

Quick hoofbeats. She stole another glance. Justin was trotting up in spite of all. A sob of relief burst from the girl. But yonder the buffalo was lowering his horns, and she knew she never would have time to mount and escape. She leveled the rifle, took steady aim and fired. The lead struck with a vicious spat square in the center of the bull's forehead. Under the impact he recoiled and shook his head but did not drop. In her excitement Sally Ann had forgotten that the thick skull of a buffalo is as impervious as a steel shield.

Off to a flank sounded more hoofbeats. Through enveloping dust shone the white hide of a horse, a trooper bent low over his neck. Yet both Peter, spurring slow old Humpty to his limit, and the watching girl knew that rescue would come too late. For again the buffalo was preparing to charge.

Major Lindsay and all the Fourth would have been proud of Sally Ann then. Coolly, never missing, she pumped four rounds into the beast before her. Each one rebounded harmlessly from his case-hardened skull. She might just as well have been using a pea-shooter.

The buffalo uttered a furious bellow and lunged forward in a thunderous charge.

Sally Ann jumped back, tripping on the hampering skirt

Sally Ann flung both arms around the neck of the trembling Justin. As the horse sprang aside, dragging her, the bull hurtled past

of her riding habit. In falling, she flung both arms around the neck of the trembling Justin. As the horse sprang aside, dragging her, the bull hurtled past.

In the fighting heart of the frustrated monster remained one last reserve of vengeful might. He whirled and charged again. In his path lay Sally Ann, helpless on the ground, her grip on Justin broken, and the horse galloping off in snorting terror.

Peter, oncoming, fired from the saddle. The range was still long, and Humpty's rocking gallop spoiled his aim. He missed by two feet.

Ahead of the desperate trooper sped a bounding form. A tawny streak flashed through the air. Fangs clamped on the muzzle of the charging bison, and staghound and buffalo struggled to the death.

Savage rumblings were still issuing from Bran's throat when he loosed his hold. The buffalo bull lay inert and lifeless, a brown mass on the prairie.

Bran trotted over to where a trooper of the Seventh held a weeping girl, her head nestled against his shoulder. The dog came and sat down beside them, fringed tail sweeping back and forth across the ground in stately approval. Peter stretched down a hand, and Bran licked it. Then Sally Ann dropped to her knees and flung her arms around the staghound's neck.

IV

A double row of wall tents, precisely aligned, had been pitched for the ladies on the night's camping ground. On the picket line, weary horses contentedly champed the oats in their feed-bags. From the cooks' fires wafted a delicious smell of buffalo meat. Sentries sniffed it as they walked their posts and counted the minutes until relief. The dogs, first to catch the aroma, had congregated in a circle around the cooking. That circle, growing gradually smaller, was repeatedly widened by a vociferous mess sergeant, only to close in again after a few minutes.

Custer, pacing up and down, wrought up by grief and repentance, was slowly being calmed by the soft and soothing words of his wife, his sister, and Sally Ann. Again he burst out in bitter self-recrimination.

"Sally Ann, I'll never forgive myself, leaving you like that, never! I'll never be able to face your mother and father."

The girl protested gently. "General, you had every reason to believe I'd be all right. And you'd have been back long before if it hadn't been for poor Maida."

Custer was having a hard time keeping command of himself. That beloved staghound of his was dead. She had leaped for the throat of a buffalo and was dragging the animal down, when a bullet in a wild fusilade from the carbines of hunting troopers had struck her in the brain.

"You loved Maida so, Autie," Elizabeth Custer said. "Nobody can blame you for delaying to see to her."

"While this dear girl of ours was almost trampled to death!" Custer exclaimed, gritting his teeth.

Margaret Calhoun rose and grasped her brother's arms. "It was another staghound that saved her, Autie," she reminded him. "Now it's over and done with. The hunt succeeded. You're the host tonight. You wouldn't want to spoil the evening for your officers and men."

"No. You're right, Maggie." Custer squared his shoulders and called: "Sergeant, mess ready? Good. Have a trumpeter sound the call."

The camp responded with a will. At board tables on a trestle, the officers' team with the higher buffalo score was toasted by the losers. Prairie night fell as the feast was finished, and stars twinkled brightly, vying with tongues of flame of the big campfire around which gathered the ladies and officers and every trooper not on guard. Peter, Bran's drowsy head resting on his thigh, gazed across at Sally Ann. The girl gazed back, and the light in her eyes seemed to shine brighter than the stars or the fire. Tonight it bothered Peter not at all that Lieutenant Trelford was sitting by her side, being ardently attentive.

A chorus of soldiers, accompanied by bandsmen with a fiddle, banjo, and concertina, sang favorite songs, comic and sentimental: *One-Hoss Shay, Susan Jane, Mother, Kiss Me in My Dreams.* The last set not a few hardened Indian-fighters to gulping and loudly blowing their noses. A sergeant, who once had starred in minstrel shows, did a lively buck-and-wing shuffle. In the following pause, Mrs. Custer rose. She had noticed her husband sinking into one of the fits of melancholy from which only she could divert him. Her soft voice was clear in the stillness, broken only by the fire's crackling.

"May I tell you a story?" she asked. "It's an old Chinese fable and it's about cavalry horses, so I think you'd all like to hear it."

"Go ahead, Libby," the General urged, lifting his head.

"Once upon a time," she began, "there was a certain King who was so miserly that for a long time his army had no cavalry, because of the high price of horses. But at last he was persuaded to buy five hundred horses as a protection against his enemies. When he had fed these horses for some time, and his kingdom was at peace with all the world, the King said to himself: 'It is costing a great deal to feed these five hundred horses. They have to be cared for all the time, and are of no use in the protection of my kingdom.' So he ordered the master of the royal stables to blind the eyes of the horses and to set them turning the mills, so that they would at least earn their living, and not be an expense to the king-dom."

A murmur of angry horror, led by Custer, ran around the circle. Few blacker crimes could be imagined by these listening cavalrymen, and the King's penury reminded them of all-too-close parallels in Government "economy," from which the Army had often suffered. When the mutter-ing died away, Elizabeth Custer gravely continued:

"After the horses had been used to turning the mills for a long time, all of a sudden a neighboring King raised troops and invaded the country. The King at once gave orders to equip the horses and provide them with harness of war, in order to provide mounts for his brave soldiers. When the hour for battle came, the soldiers whipped and spurred their horses to drive them forward against the enemy and break his ranks. But when the horses felt the whip and spur, they began turning round and round in a circle, and refused to go forward. The enemy's troops quickly saw that the cavalry was good for nothing. So they marched against it and quickly crushed the King's whole army."

"Served that blamed King right!" Custer called out.

"Hope he got scalped fust crack!" a trooper shouted.

Mrs. Custer turned to Sally Ann. "Sing us a song, dear," she begged.

The girl reached behind her for her guitar. She strummed several chords, mellow and haunting in the calm stillness of the night. The embers of the dying campfire reflected a rosy glow on her lovely face. A sigh rustled through the listening ring. In that moment, to every man there the girl was the sweetheart he had won or lost in his youth. Sally Ann's clear voice lifted in *Annie Laurie*.

> *Maxwelton's braes are bonnie,*
> *Where early fa's the dew,*

And 'twas there that Annie Laurie
Gave me her promise true......

Peter bent forward, arms around his knees, his heart full. Beside him, Bran's ears were up, as if he sensed an echo from the land of his forebears. MacTavish behind them unashamedly wiped tears from his eyes with the back of his hand.

The tender, sweet soprano soared in the refrain.

Which ne'er forgot will be,
And for bonnie Annie Laurie
I'd lay me down and dee.

Fervent applause resounded as the song ended. Through the succeeding silence, Trelford's voice carried. Leaning toward Sally Ann, the officer gallantly declared:

"If Annie Laurie was anything like the girl who just sang about her, I'd 'lay me down and dee' for her, too."

The gruff tones of MacTavish cut in quickly.

"The mon didna get Annie, after a'."

15: MARCHING MIRAGE

PAY DAY

I

A GALLOPING courier met the hunting cavalcade on its march back to the post. Along the column ran an electric thrill. No one needed to be told that the long-awaited orders had come at last. Custer and Cooke spurred back to Fort Abe, while the rest of the party pushed after them.

General Terry, commander of the entire expedition, already had arrived. A veteran leader in the struggle between the States, the tall, bearded general had seen no Indian-fighting and he warmly greeted Custer on whose experience he greatly relied. As the hunters reached the post, other troops assigned to compose the column with the 7th Cavalry came marching in—sturdy infantry, guards for the wagon train : two companies of the Seventeenth, one of the Sixth, and a detail from the Twentieth, manning a platoon of three horse-drawn Gatling guns.

It was these pioneer machine-guns, invented by Dr. Richard Jordan Gatling in 1861, which drew the fascinated interest of most of the cavalrymen on the post. Mounted on a small carriage, each boasted ten barrels, fed from a cartridge belt. A bearded gunner proudly showed them off to Peter and others crowding around.

"Somehows we never used 'em against the Rebs," the gunner said. "The Frenchies did in their scrap with the Prooshians a few years ago but not enough—they got licked. All you does is turn this here crank and sweeps her barrel from side to side. She shoots four hundred rounds a minute. Man, she mows 'em down like a scythe. Trouble is, all they give us to pull 'em is danged old plugs—condemned cavalry hosses."

"You'll be all right with the infantry, but how are you going to keep up with us—with cavalry—when we have to move fast?" Peter asked.

The gunner disgustedly spat a stream of tobacco juice. "*You* tell me, Corp," he suggested.

Peter was oppressed by an uneasy feeling of opportunity given and tossed away. What was a volley from single-shot carbines compared to a stream of lead from those three Gatlings—1200 shots a minute—against a mass of charging Sioux?

On still another score he knew vague disquiet. That was when Custer's order came down that sabres would not be carried on this campaign. There was reason for it, of course. Swords were an encumbering extra weight; their rattling betrayed you to an alert enemy. Yet Peter well remembered how the *arme blanche* had stood him in good stead in the Fourth's fights on the Staked Plains when his revolver was emptied and his carbine useless in a mêlée, with Comanches clutching at his bridle. The day of the sabre might be over, but it was good to have its hilt in your hand as a last resort. Custer, consistently, would leave behind his own trophy sword, its Damascus blade inscribed with the legend: "Draw me not without cause. Sheathe me not without honor."

Wagons loaded at the Quartermaster and Commissary storehouses. Officers and non-coms barked orders.

" 'D' Company will draw ammunition at 4. One hundred rounds per man" . . . "First platoon, lead down to the blacksmith shop and get your nags shod" . . . "Oil up that leather. Want yer stirrup strap to break in charge, do yuh?" . . . "Get the saddler to pad that there saddle so it don't rest on that gall. If it turns inta a sore, rookie, the Cap'n'll make yuh walk the hull campaign!" . . . "Check your equipment. Blanket roll, overcoat, shelter tent, tin cup, canteen, haversack, lariat, picket pin. Got 'em? You better have!" . . . "Got a jack-knife? Naw, not for whittlin' nor pickin' yer teeth, neither. S'posin' a big buck Injun comes ridin' down on yuh an' yuh miss him with yer fust round and the cartridge jams. I'm tellin' yuh, yuh want a knife to clear that breach quick."

All day long the trumpets blasted with brazen urgency. The crowded post throbbed with preparations. A detachment of Arickara scouts under their chief, Bloody Knife, arrived and camped noisily. The dogs, certain of what was afoot, raced about excitedly or stationed themselves beside piles of equipment, determined not to be left behind. Most of the pack would be disappointed. Custer had instructed Mac-Tavish that only five lucky ones would be allowed to accompany the column: Tuck, Swift, Lady, Kaiser, and Bran.

Only toward "Tattoo" did the post quiet down, and it was

then that Eliza sought out Corporal-Trumpeter Shannon.

"*She* want to see you," the cook announced.

"Mrs. Custer?" Peter questioned, hoping otherwise.

White teeth flashed in the smiling face. "Young sojer, you knows better. Ain't Miss Libby. You come right along."

He found Sally Ann beside the Custer quarters. The meeting was distressingly public, with officers and orderlies hurrying by.

"Pete, dear," the girl said, "this isn't good-by. The General is going to let me ride out tomorrow with Mrs. Custer and Mrs. Calhoun, along with the column as far as the first camp. I'll see you then. This is to ask you a great favor. I want you to ride Justin on this campaign. Leave that slow old Humpty in the stable."

"Sally Ann sweetheart, I'd give anything if I had Justin under me. But you know the music has to ride grays. That's not just because it's a tradition and Custer's preference. He says that in action he has to be able to spot his trumpeters quick, and a gray or white horse stands out."

"Stands out for Indian sharpshooters, too, Pete. Oh, you've just got to take Justin! You know that in a fight a good horse can mean the difference between life and death."

"I know, but I'll be all right. Sally Ann, three columns are converging on the Sioux. I swear the Seventh can lick 'em alone."

"You're riding Justin, Corporal Shannon, and that's an order. I'll get it from the General himself."

"Sally Ann, no! I can't let you bother him, with all he's got to do. You mustn't ask him, either—you're an Army girl. No, my dearest."

"Oh, Peter!"

"Tattoo" sounded. Peter called, "See you tomorrow," and ran for the barracks.

II

Men marching forth to war. It is a centuries-old spectacle, countless times repeated, yet never failing to stir pulses, to tug at heartstrings. Sally Ann as an Army girl had witnessed it often. Today it thrilled her as never before.

Whooping, the "Ree" scouts dashed off in the van, decked in barbaric finery. After them rode Custer's trusted civilian scout, the melancholy Charley Reynolds, and the halfbreed scout and interpreter, Mitch Bouyer, who knew the country ahead like the back of his hand. There strode the infantry with the Gatlings, bronze barrels gleaming in the sun. Beside the long wagon train rode the correspondent, Mark Kellogg, astride a gray mule, though Sherman's orders expressly had forbade Custer taking a newspaperman. Boston Custer, a younger brother of the General, and Autie Reed, a nephew, helped herd the beef cattle. With the General, Captain Tom, and Lieutenant Calhoun, their brother-in-law, five members of the Custer family were taking the field.

Now, to the blare of martial music, to the lilting strains of its own *Garryowen,* paraded the Seventh in column of platoons. General Terry had ordered that it be last to leave its own post, to give the married men an opportunity to fall out, dismount and say farewell. A long, rippling current of Army blue, all twelve companies present, six hundred strong, and its head Lieutenant Colonel, Brevet Major General George Armstrong Custer, gallantly debonair, as always, in campaign buckskin and sombrero but with golden locks shorn close this time.

The face of the commander of the Seventh gleamed with pride in the troops he headed. No bandbox soldiers, these. If any foreign observers had been present—super-military Germans, white-and-gold hussars of Austria, Britishers, smart in scarlet—they might have looked askance at these

American cavalrymen. Campaign hats were jammed down on bronzed brows, bandanas knotted around necks. Their carbines were slung over loose blue tunics, and holstered revolvers swung at cartridge belts. The stripes of cavalry yellow along breeches of officers and non-coms disappeared into black, spurred boots. Overcoat, blanket roll, and other gear were strapped to the pommels and cantles of McClellan saddles, and saddle-bags bulked with rations and ammunition. Yet in all our conflicts there never has been such a dashing, picturesque figure as the rough-and-ready, hard-bitten trooper of the Indian wars.

A casual glance would not have noted the flaws in this formidable array of fighting men. That the companies were below strength. That more than a third of the regiment was recruits, untested in battle. That only twenty-eight out of its complement of forty-one officers rode with it, reducing each outfit to one or two officers. All this Custer and the other veterans knew and, good soldiers, could only accept.

Sally Ann's brown eyes swept the column, caught the yellow corporal's chevrons on the sleeve of a blue-clad trooper on the right of the front rank of massed trumpeters and clung there. Trelford and other young officers saluted her as they rode past. She waved but hardly saw them. She was weeping like the other women around her when the band struck up *The Girl I Left Behind Me,* but quickly dried her tears. She was one of the fortunate three who would be given one more glimpse. As the rear of the regiment cleared the post, she mounted Justin and joined Mrs. Custer and Maggie Calhoun, ready to overtake the column.

Then as the dust masked the departing regiment, the girl beheld a sight which would linger with her all her life. The clouds suddenly reflected a vivid, moving panorama, one of the rare mirages of the plains. It mirrored the procession of men and horses—the 7th Cavalry streaming across the sky—flowing steadily on—swinging through illimitable space—riding on until the blue horsemen faded from view, as if the halls of Valhalla, hereafter of warriors, had swallowed them forever.

III

The three Army women, under the escort of the paymaster and his guard, soon overtook the column. Since the start had been made late in the day, it became necessary to halt for the night camp after only a short march.

"Guidons forward," the trumpets sang. Guidon-bearers left their companies to ride ahead and form behind the color sergeant, carrying Custer's own guidon of red and blue. The detail galloped briskly ahead. Where each company was to encamp, its guidon-bearer lifted his banneret from stirrup socket and thrust its pointed metal butt into the ground.

Rapidly the camp took form. Trumpeters sounded "Pay Day," and each company lined up in turn at the table where the paymaster sat, his valise crammed with greenbacks. First sergeants called rolls, and company commanders checked the amount due. Many a trooper, saluting and taking his two-months' pay, turned away grumbling and griping. "Sure and what's a man to do with money out here? Feed it to thim prairie dogs?" It was by General Terry's order that pay day had been postponed from yesterday. If paid on the post, too many soldiers would have squandered every dollar in drunken sprees in Bismarck, and the start of the march would have found the guard-house crammed with sodden wrecks, unfit for duty.

Peter hurried away from the pay table to say good-by to Sally Ann, for the ladies were due to ride back to the post any minute now. Surely Sally Ann would make an opportunity for them to meet, difficult though it would be for her to break away from the young officers and bid farewell to a trooper.

Nowhere could he find her. But yonder he sighted a vanishing little cloud of dust. The ladies had left.

He thought he never had known such keenly bitter disappointment, such shattering disillusionment. He could face no one—he had to be alone. Head sunken on his chest, he wandered down to the comparative solitude of the Headquarters picket line. As he approached it, he halted abruptly. In the midst of the line of grays, a black hide stood out like a blot of ink on white paper.

Justin lifted his white-blazed forehead and nickered a welcome. There was a note fastened to his halter.

"Pete (ran Sally Ann's hasty scrawl), now you'll have to ride Justin. Mrs. Custer helped me, Scotty changed saddles, and I've taken Humpty. We had to rush off before the General found out. He didn't notice, he was having such a hard time saying good-by to Mrs. C. This is why I couldn't say good-by to you. Justin will bring you back safe to me, Pete dearest. All, all my love. Sally Ann."

Custer did notice the next morning, after he had finished sending a detachment ahead on a scout. His eyes were cold as they scanned his corporal-trumpeter's black mount.

"What in Tophet are you doing on that horse, Corporal?" he barked. "Get your own mount at once."

"Couldn't find him, sir."

"Couldn't find him! Confound it, what do you mean by that?"

"No explanation, sir."

"Why—" Custer's scowl slowly dissolved into a grin. "I get it. Somebody left a changeling on the picket line. I might have expected it. That girl! That Army brat!

"That's 'a horse of another color,' eh? Maybe it's

better to have you mounted on a good horse than a white plug. Too late to do anything about it now. That girl counted on that. All right, Shannon, sound 'The General.' We're moving out."

IV

On marched the column, advance-, flank-, and rear-guards out. Long marches, forced marches—some thirty miles a day. Marches under sunny skies, through rain and mud, even a late snowstorm. Marches where Custer rode twice as far as any other, galloping up and down the column or far across the prairie, the staghounds bounding beside him.

As always, Custer's gallant figure, straight in the saddle as he swung across the prairie, fired Peter's imagination. Watching the General gallop toward the horizon, Peter told himself: He doesn't belong here and now. He has ridden out of the past—out of feudal times—out of some medieval romance. Yonder astride his charger, his staghounds at his heels, and we, his men-at-arms, in his train, he ought to be leading a Crusade instead of an Indian campaign. We ought to be marching against Saracens, not the Sioux. It came to Peter suddenly that George Armstrong Custer was another Richard *Cœur de Lion,* with both the Lion-Hearted's virtues and his faults.

That was the resemblance he had almost caught that night back at Fort Abe when he had laid hands on one of the *Waverley* novels. There was likely to be one or two of Sir Walter Scott's books in the scant store at a frontier post—on a shelf at the sutler's or in some officer's cherished library. It was *The Talisman* he'd been reading, an exciting yarn. Roswal, the staghound in it, keeping watch by Richard's royal standard with his master, Sir Kenneth, was Bran's image. "From time to time he lowered his lofty head and wagged his tail, as his master passed and repassed him in the short turns which he took upon his post; or when the knight stood silent and abstracted leaning on his lance and looking up toward heaven, his faithful attendant ventured sometimes, in the phrase of romance, 'to disturb his thoughts,' and awaken him from his reveries, by thrusting his large, rough snout into the knight's gauntleted hand, to solicit a transitory caress."

Best was that dramatic moment in the story when Roswal attacked Richard's enemy, the villainous Conrade, rushing in to leap upon Conrade's charger, seizing the Marquis by the throat and pulling him down from the saddle. Conrade's followers had clamored, "Cut the dog to pieces," but Richard had ringingly replied, "He dies the death who injures the hound. He hath but done his duty, after the sagacity with which God and nature have endowed the brave animal." Yes, that was Custer to the life.

Peter saw the General come galloping back, Bran and the other hounds around him. Surely he was another Richard the Lion-Hearted. Or was he more like Roland who died so gloriously with Charlemagne's rear-guard, fighting the Saracens in the pass at Roncesvalles? It came upon Peter with a cold qualm that only death on the battlefield—like Roland's—was lacking to complete Custer's already legendary fame.

But battle seemed further distant, more unlikely every day. May dwindled into June, and still no signs of Indians. On pressed the column—the companies of matched bays, sorrels, blacks, chestnuts, grays—the foot-slogging infantry—the creaking wagon train. Still the trumpets began and closed the day. Tents rose and were struck. Campfires flared and died down. Horses and mules were watered, fed, and picketed. Mess, the glow of pipes, tired troopers pillowing their heads on saddles. "Reveille" and another march.

The Seventh hardened under the steady grind, but trouble developed within the column itself. And that trouble was mules—not the veteran jugheads hauling the wagons but pack-mules.

Soon now the wagon train would have to be left behind with the infantry, while the cavalry pushed ahead. To catch the Sioux the Seventh would have to move fast, and only led pack-mules, carrying the rations and ammunition, could keep up. Mules suitable for pack had been driven along with the column, a whole braying, rambunctious herd of them but the Seventh was sadly ignorant of their handling, a serious defect in its training. It had to learn as it marched.

A few experienced packers strove mightily, instructing troopers on packing an *aparejo*, how to throw a diamond hitch and make the load fast. But mule-packing is an art not to be casually acquired. Fumbling cavalrymen struggled with the shavetails, which, knowing them for the amateurs they were, became proverbially stubborn. Blindfolded, the beasts accepted their burdens, but when the blinds were whisked off—then tribulation and turmoil. Loads slipped and fell off during every march, with kicking, cavorting animals scattering over the plains. Some mules could not be used at all. Affairs came to such a pass that substitutes for them had to be taken from the wagon mules. As a last resort, Old Pizen was taken out of his team, replaced and tried under pack.

Peter rashly volunteered to assist in the experiment. Jake Small, the teamster, regarded the trumpeter morosely and shook his head.

"Pete, won't you never learn?" he demanded. "You're like the first feller who ever fooled with gunpowder and touched a match to a mess of it for to see what'd happen. Man, man!"

Peter grinned and persisted. Jake had kept the mule race harness and stowed it under his wagon seat. With the aid of that contrivance, Old Pizen was successfully packed and proved an astonishing success. On his first trial march, Peter on Justin led the mule, jauntily carrying two cases of ammunition. Cheers ran along the column as Peter moved ahead at a trot, with Old Pizen following docilely, not even tugging back at the lead-rope. Bran, plainly just as proud of the feat, capered along beside his long-eared friend. Peter glanced back fondly at his "tow."

"Pizen, you old rapscallion, you," he said, "you keep cropping up all through my service, don't you? Can't I ever get rid of you?"

The mule flipped one ear toward him and snorted. Peter laughed. "Not yet, you say?"

Not many days later, on a certain hill, Peter would vividly remember that jocular remark of his. He was far from being through with Old Pizen.

Peter turned the mule over to the pack-master and returned to his duty as trumpeter. The column forged on. It pushed westward through the Bad Lands, crossed the little Missouri, approached the Powder River. Peter began to notice that General Custer seemed strangely depressed— Custer who was always exhilarated by the prospect of action.

A sense of foreboding began to grow on the trumpeter as he sat before a fire when the night camp had been made. Bran rested his head on his master's knee and vainly begged for a pat. Justin fared no better when he came up behind his rider and stamped. Not until he gently tapped Peter's shoulder with one white forefoot did the black Morgan win his customary evening nibble of hardtack.

Peter stared moodily toward Custer's tent, where the General's own red and blue flag with its silver crossed sabres snapped in the wind. A sudden gust, and the flag was blown down. Peter watched Lieutenant Godfrey, who was passing, stop to pick up the flag and drive its ferule deep into the ground. He shivered a little. It was foolishly superstitious of him, he knew, but he could not dismiss the thought that he had witnessed a bad omen.

However, before he fell asleep that night, Peter had thrown off his melancholy. The warmth of Bran, crouched beside him, was grateful. As he commenced to drowse, another staghound in a book of Scott's, *The Abbot,* came into his mind and merged into a dream. In Peter's vision the deerhound Wolf of the tale became Bran, and the charming Lady of Avenel was transformed into Sally Ann. Vividly he saw the two of them, Bran sitting at Sally Ann's feet and gazing up adoringly at her while she spoke to the dog in the words of Scott's heroine.

" 'Wolf,' she said, as if the animal could have understood her complaints, 'thou art a noble and beautiful animal; but, alas! the love and affection that I long to bestow, is of a higher quality than can fall to thy share, though I love thee much.' "

It was a pity to be aroused from such a dream, but an insistent, eerie sound dragged Peter back to consciousness. Bran was gone from his side. He raised himself on an elbow and listened. In the high wind it was faint yet unmistakable. The staghounds were howling.

Peter threw off his blankets and walked toward the strange keening. Bran and the others, muzzles up, were gathered at Custer's tent.

"Be still. Come awa'."

That was MacTavish's voice in the darkness. Peter helped him lead the dogs off and tie them.

"Wae!" Fergus whispered mournfully in his friend's ear. " 'Tis a fule notion to some, nae doot, but there's nae Scot but kens that staghounds hae second sight. Ay, their eyes see what mon canna. And, Peter, they howl when they sight the Death Angel."

16: THE RENEGADE

THE RED HUSSARS

I

THE vast camp of the Sioux and Cheyennes spread across
the valley of the Little Big Horn, tepees pitched in six great
circles according to tribal divisions. Boys drove the pony

herds to drink from the river or let them crop the rich grass from the hillsides. Smoke curled up from the fires where squaws cooked the meat brought in by hunters who had ranged far, since game had grown scarce in the vicinity of so large an assembly.

Here was massed the might of the Sioux nation and the Northern Cheyennes—from ten to twelve thousand men, women, and children, from which the war chiefs had mustered nearly three thousand warriors. Here ruled wily old Sitting Bull, chief of the Uncpapa Sioux, making medicine and bestowing gifts. And here the valiant war chiefs, Crazy Horse and Gall and Crow King and Rain-in-the-Face, led the scalp dances and welcomed new recruits streaming in from the reservations. Here was savage strength unprecedented, unsuspected by the paleface. Let his soldiers come—the red man was unafraid.

Already Crazy Horse had dealt with one blue column. He had shattered General Crook's advance guard, then struck his main body at the Rosebud, fought him to a standstill and forced the renowned Gray Fox to retreat to his base. There had been brushes with Gibbon's troops, too, and the scalps of soldiers hung drying in the sun. Custer, with a third column, was coming on, but even the dreaded Yellow Hair now left the Sioux undaunted.

Through the camp moved a single white man. Although he had stained his skin and dressed as an Indian, there was no mistaking his Caucasian features, and through vanity he had not dyed his auburn hair. A bodyguard of two braves accompanied him, to identify him as a friend in the event of a meeting with strange warriors. Otherwise he walked free, and in his tepee he was waited on by two young squaws who had replaced the white woman, a settler's daughter, he had discarded some months ago.

Former Corporal Rick, deserter from the 4th U.S.

Cavalry, was well satisfied with himself. Never had he heard of another white man who was admitted as he was to the high councils of the Sioux. Small wonder they held him in esteem. They owed many of their rifles and much ammunition to this shrewd, unscrupulous trader who had connections with every crooked Indian agent and storekeeper in the territory. As a one-time cavalryman, he was able to give valuable advice to the Indians on the probable tactics of their enemies. For Crazy Horse, Rick had more than once interpreted news brought in by scouts. The hostiles were far better informed on the three Army columns in the field against them than were any of the generals, from Terry down, on the strength and movements of the Sioux.

In his progress through the camp, the white trader admiringly regarded the thronging warriors. They were fighting men, these Sioux and Cheyennes, as tough or tougher than the Comanches and Kiowas he had tackled when he rode with the 4th Cavalry. To them war was the breath of life, a rite, the proof of manhood. That they had grievances aplenty, that they were warring to preserve their independence, even for existence, seemed secondary reasons. It's true, thought Rick, that they've got some fool ideas. They make a ceremony out of a battle. They stop to take a scalp when they might be killing another soldier. They rush in to touch the body of an enemy with a stick, counting coup, and get themselves shot while they're doing it. A lot of the time it's every warrior for himself, and they don't take to discipline. But they're bang-up cavalry and they've got a cracking good general in Crazy Horse. He's already shown he can lead 'em. He's whipped Crook, one of the best the Army's got.

Rick, striding toward the lodge of Sitting Bull, carried himself with the arrogance his position permitted, but his eyes were wary and calculating as always. Confident as he was of an Indian victory in the forthcoming battles, he was too astute not to forsee the inevitable aftermath. No matter how notable the triumph, this great concourse would melt away, some tribesmen returning to the reservations, others riding over the border into Canada.

That would be Rick's own route of escape when the time came—Canada. Across the line, he would go white again. Everything was prepared there. In several banks he had sizable deposits. Selling arms to the Indians was a highly profitable game, and other deals of his since he had skipped out from the Fourth and gone "over the hill" had proved no less so. Everything he touched had brought him in money. His luck had run strong at the gambling tables of the mining camps. And that had been a real haul he had made that night in the Black Hills, when he waylaid a prospector who had struck it rich, murdered him in his sleep and appropriated a fat sack of gold nuggets.

Joining the Sioux in the fight ahead would be his last exploit, the renegade assured himself. Having entered the camp, he could not safely leave until after the battle. He was perfectly aware of the risk to which he had committed himself and knew it for a needless one. Yet he had been unable to forego a part in the shattering defeat he confidently expected would be the fate of the Army he hated.

Of one thing more Rick was certain—the Army would never lay hands on him again. He had seen what happened to captured deserters. They would force him back into the uniform he loathed and shave off his auburn hair right down to the skull. A provost guard would march him out in front of the whole regiment, drawn up on parade. A sergeant would rip off his chevrons and cut and yank the U. S. buttons from his blouse, while the adjutant read orders publishing his disgrace. Then with the fifes shrilling "The Rogue's March," they'd cram his "bobtail" dishonorable discharge into his pocket and drum him out of camp. They'd either do that or shoot him—and Rick preferred the firing squad.

His lips curled back from his teeth as, answering a summons, he entered the lodge of Sitting Bull where the chiefs were met in council.

II

Rick took his place in the circle. The wrinkled copper visages of the old chiefs and the fierce, eagle-like faces of the war chiefs turned toward him. They questioned him about Custer, and there was awe and respect in their voices when they spoke of the formidable Yellow Hair.

Rick sneered. Why were his red brothers so troubled about Custer? He was only another soldier who could be tricked and beaten by the bold and resolute. Why he, Rick himself, had fooled Yellow Hair and slipped out of his hands one day in White Wolf's lodge.

Would Custer fight? they asked.

Rick answered confidently. Certainly Custer would fight. His reputation was at stake. But did not the Sioux outnumber him five to one? And let the chiefs remember Yellow Hair's favorite tactic—that which he had used at the Washita and elsewhere—his custom of dividing his command before he attacked. Let the chiefs strike each column separately and crush it as they had Crook.

Grunts of approval ran around the circle. Then the chiefs demanded: "Get us more guns."

That now was impossible, Rick declared. He stared them boldly in the eye and said: "Let my brothers take them from dead soldiers."

As the council prepared to adjourn, Rick rose and spoke once more.

"One small favor, my brothers. If any warrior takes alive

one of the trumpeters of the soldiers—one of those who blows a horn—let him be given into my hands. There is a certain one who is my enemy. Let me deal with him."

Sitting Bull nodded assent. "Let it be done."

17: EVE OF BATTLE

OFFICERS' CALL

I

PETER stood and ground his teeth at an order which had come down from Headquarters, as countless soldiers have done over countless orders in every army in history.

Toward mid-June, the Seventh had made camp at the confluence of the Powder and Yellowstone rivers. This, orders stated, would be the column's base. The wagon train would remain here under guard, with pack-mules taking over the transport. Even the band was to be left, while the regiment it was wont to play into action marched on. Those steps, Peter conceded, were necessary in a fast-moving campaign.

It was the command, verbally given to MacTavish, that aroused the trumpeter's bitter resentment. The staghounds must remain in camp also.

Whether the decision to leave the hounds behind was Custer's or General Terry's, Peter did not know. Of course, it was true that dogs were no longer used in warfare. The time was long past when the Romans launched their savage Molossian hounds, trained to attack, on barbarian hordes, or when dogs in armor followed the Crusaders and joined them in battle to wrest the Holy Land from the infidel. On this continent—so Peter's father had written him when he first learned about Bran—Cortez and the Conquistadores had sent their fierce greyhounds into the fray against the Aztec Indians, but that was three and a half centuries ago. Today "let slip the dogs of war" was just a phrase you read in Shakespeare.

On second thought Peter calmed down somewhat. After all, it was humane to avoid exposing these fine animals to death or wounds from Sioux bullet, lance, or war club. But Peter knew that both Custer and he would sorely miss them; he had not appreciated until now how much he depended upon Bran as a faithful and vigilant bodyguard.

It was no easy parting. Where MacTavish, furious that he must stay behind in charge of the hounds, was tying them securely to wagon wheels, Peter said his farewell to Bran. The tawny staghound reared himself up on his hind legs and placed his forepaws on his master's shoulders. So large now that, erect, he could almost look levelly into Peter's face, the great hound, understanding without question what was in the air, pleaded eloquently with his eyes. Words could not have said more plainly, "Master, take me with you. With all my love of you, I beg you do not leave me."

The trumpeter put his arms around Bran's shaggy neck and laid his head against the hound's, as one might embrace an old comrade.

"No. Bran, I can't," he answered in a voice he strove to keep from breaking. "Wait here for me. I'll be back."

Trumpets called, companies swung up into their saddles, and the Seventh rode on. Five staghounds, whining and whimpering, strained mightily at their leashes. As the blue column marched away across the sage-strewn plain, General Custer turned to gaze backward toward where the sound of lamenting hounds still could be heard. He saw that his trumpeter was looking back also. When Peter faced forward again, his eyes met the General's. A message passed between them—the pledged fellowship of men who love dogs.

MacTavish, wise in the ways of his charges, did not release them all that day nor even when night fell, but returned to the wagons from time to time to make certain that they were still well secured. In the morning he was up early to feed them. Four staghounds greeted him with wagging tails. Where the fifth had been tied remained only a tough halter rope, gnawed in two. Bran was gone.

II

The game of hide-and-seek the Seventh was playing with the Sioux was growing hot. Major Reno, who had been sent on a scout with his battalion, returned and reported that he had discovered a broad Indian trail leading toward the valley of the Little Big Horn. No small war party but only a large assemblage could have marked the prairie with so many travois ruts and imprinted such numerous hoofmarks. Surely a band of that size would stand and fight; in any event, it would find escape more difficult.

But Reno had missed a vital piece of information. Not forty miles from where he rode, those same Indians had struck and repulsed General Crook. This highly important news would not be learned until days later, and the failure of the three Army columns in the field to keep in touch laid them open to disaster. The brilliant Chief Crazy Horse already had taken advantage of that isolation to hurl Crook back, and now was biding his time to catch another blue force alone and shatter it.

General Terry, after receiving Reno's report of an Indian concentration, led the 7th Cavalry onward to the junction of the Yellowstone and Rosebud rivers. There, at any rate, the plan of campaign worked as scheduled, for General Gibbon and his troops had arrived at that designated rendezvous, and two of the Army columns met.

Terry called Custer and Gibbon aboard the river steamboat, *Far West,* which had brought supplies for the troops up the Yellowstone. In a cabin, the commander-in-chief issued final orders to his two subordinates. They were to march, separately, on the valley of the Little Big Horn—he, Terry, remaining with Gibbon and leaving the more experienced Indian-fighter, Custer, on his own. Reaching the valley, where by every indication they would find the enemy encamped, the two blue columns were to close in and crush the Indians between the jaws of pincers in smashing attacks.

Rumors, most of them astonishingly accurate, began to spread like wildfire through the Seventh's bivouac that evening, even before Custer ordered "Officers' Call" sounded. Every knot of troopers buzzed with talk.

"We're off and after 'em tomorrow, me b'ys." . . . "Gibbon and his outfit hikes up the other bank of the Rosebud and us up this un. We'll catch them Injuns atween us." . . . "You-all like to put up a little bet Old Curley don't get theah fustest and keep the whole shootin'-match to himself?" . . . "Donnerwetter! Dey try to gif de Oldt Man a whole pattalion uf de 2nd Cafalry to come along mit us and he von't haf 'em." . . . "Sure and he knows the Seventh can lick them redskins by itself, Dutchy." . . . "Why won't Custer take them Gatlings, though?" . . . "Aw, them old plugs hauling 'em is too slow."

Peter, listening, knitted his brows in worriment. There was such a thing as overconfidence. It seemed plain that Custer was expected to co-operate with Gibbon, but probably the former's orders gave him considerable freedom of action, for even Peter, though only a trumpeter, had been able to sense the trust Terry placed in the Seventh's commander. But would Custer wait or attack alone? Considering his reputation, his impulsive nature, and the urgency he must feel to square himself with authorities in Washington, it was hard not to bet on the second alternative.

Peter chided himself. A trooper ought not to feel any doubts of so gallant and able a commanding officer. But when he scanned the faces of the officers emerging from Custer's tent after the call, he could not shake off those doubts. They had found Custer still in the grip of a strange depression and they looked puzzled and downcast.

Despite the gray rawness of the next morning, Peter's misgivings vanished, for the Seventh was mounting up to ride toward battle. Yonder Generals Terry and Gibbon sat their saddles to review the march past. The wind flaunted the bright folds of the regimental standard and Custer's own guidon of red, blue and silver, staffs grasped firmly by color sergeants. What if the band was not present to play the regiment by with *Garryowen?* Peter and the other trumpeters, massed, raised their instruments to their lips and blew a stirring paean. Company after company, scouts, pack train, streamed by. Custer, eyes bright with pride, turned out to salute the reviewing officers.

Good-by and good luck, they bade him. And Gibbon called out:

"Now, Custer, don't be greedy, but wait for us."

The dashing figure in buckskin wheeled his horse, waved and shouted back, "No, I won't."

You could, thought Peter, take that two ways.

III

The gait of the black Morgan, Justin, was smooth as always. His hoofs, thudding on the prairie, merged in that rhythmic tattoo which is drummed by a cavalry regiment at the trot. A trooper was fortunate to have such a grand horse under him, Peter reminded himself for the hundredth time. He felt the reassuring weight of his carbine, revolver, and slung trumpet and knew himself to be better than competent in handling these tools of the soldier's trade.

A man could be proud to ride with the 7th U.S. Cavalry, the best—well, one of the two best regiments in the service. (Peter could not forget his loyalty to the Fourth.) Proud also to follow the gallant and honorable profession of arms, and to stand ready to fight for your country as long as she must wage wars or be prepared against them.

Action ahead—no question of it now. Peter felt the same old tingling of the spine, and his palms were clammy. Veteran though he was, he knew it would always be the same. Some few men faced battle stolidly, some with fierce exhilaration, most with inner dread. Peter knew he was numbered among the last. He remembered a passage from the Book of Judges his father had recited to him. How Gideon was about to lead a host against the Midianites when the Lord spoke to him, saying: "The people that are with thee are too many to give the Midianites into their hands, lest Israel vaunt themselves against Me, saying, Mine own hand hath saved me. Now therefore go to, proclaim in the ears of the people, saying, Whosoever is fearful and afraid, let him return and depart early from Mount Gilead. And there returned of the people twenty and two thousand; and there remained ten thousand."

John Shannon had grinned and remarked: "Pete, you can bet that practically all of the ten thousand who remained were scared, too, and just wouldn't admit it. That's the way it is when you go into a scrap. Never be ashamed of being afraid, son. We all have been. You'll find courage within you when you need it."

Peter had found that courage in past battles and believed he would again. He could not betray the trust of his father, former captain of Union cavalry, nor let down his own comrades of the Seventh. Neither could you disgrace yourself in your girl's eyes, especially if she were an Army girl. Peter was certain that, no matter how much Sally Ann loved him, she could not forgive nor forget cowardice in the face of the enemy. She might pretend to—she had heard how even a brave man's nerve broke sometimes—but it would be only a pretense. Like many a soldier before him, Peter told himself: If my nerve doesn't hold, it would be better not to come back.

Uplifted arms signaled a sudden halt. The regiment had struck the half-mile-wide trail of an Indian village on the march, the trail reported by Major Reno. Hard and fast it rode ahead—three days of forced marches—following that trail. Now, scouts declared, the path led beyond doubt into the valley of the Little Big Horn.

Custer stood at the crossroads of his career, a vital decision before him. Should he turn aside from the trail and wait for Gibbon, as his orders required, and perhaps allow the Indians to escape? Or should he thrust ahead? Yonder beckoned opportunity, opportunity for a great victory which would belong to Custer and the Seventh alone, a triumph which would burnish bright again honor and glory won so often in the past. For a commander who struck and conquered, disregard of orders was forgotten.

Peter would always remember the sweeping gesture which marked Custer's decision. The buckskin-clad arm shot up, swept forward and down. "Forward, ho," and the Seventh rode straight along that broad trail toward the valley.

A night march on June 24th brought the regiment close to the divide separating the Rosebud and Little Big Horn rivers. At dawn, scouts called Custer to the crest. Many Indians down there in the valley, they warned him—too many. The General's keen eyesight, aided by field glasses, could not confirm what the scouts reported. He knew only that hostiles had been sighted in his rear, proof that the Indians were aware of his arrival. For Yellow Hair it was now or never. Strike now, or let the Indians escape.

George Armstrong Custer was never a man to draw back from a fight. All his depression vanished. He summoned his officers for battle orders. They heard his second fateful decision: to divide his regiment into three columns. Five companies would go with Custer, three were assigned to Reno, and three to Benteen, who would be followed by the twelfth company, detailed to guard the pack-train. Just as at the Washita, they would charge the Indian camp from three sides.

Intently, Peter watched the battalions form. Into the column behind the General rode the companies he had picked, the companies of his favorite commanders: Tom Custer's troopers, Keogh's, Yates', Smith's, Calhoun's. Well, the choice was Custer's right. His young brother Boston, his nephew, and Correspondent Kellogg joined them. Then Peter heard his own name called by Lieutenant Cooke.

"Shannon, it's not your turn on the roster today," the adjutant said. "Voss is up but his English is none too good.

The General wants you. You'll serve as his trumpeter today."

"Right, sir." Peter grinned and trotted Justin over to his post behind Custer.

Forward! Beat of hoofs on the prairie and jangling accouterments. Down into the valley, cut by a river and deep gullies, rode the 7th Cavalry. Its three columns swung apart and disappeared from each other's view.

18: "TOO MANY INDIANS"

COMMENCE FIRING

I

MAJOR RENO and his men splashed through a ford to the west bank of the little Big Horn River, ranks crowding up on each other when thirsty horses could not be denied a drink. Impatiently, troopers jerked up the heads of dripping, snorting mounts, and the column threaded through a gloomy defile. As it emerged, the great Indian village in the valley spread before startled eyes. And in front of it, seeming to sprout from the very ground like sown dragon's teeth, sprang up a whooping, shooting horde of Sioux and Cheyennes.

One look, and Reno sent a galloper, then another to find Custer, who had promised to support him "with the whole outfit." Neither rider ever would be seen again.

Then the major rose in his stirrups and shouted: "Left front into line. Gallop. Guide right." Fours swung abreast, and the blue array thundered down on the red—112 men charging thousands.

The frantic horses of three troopers took their bits in their teeth and dashed ahead, straight into the Indian mass. It swallowed up one rider without a trace. Miraculously the other two ran that deadly gantlet, got their mounts under control and, bleeding from wounds, rejoined the battalion. But now the tossing red sea threatened to engulf the entire command. It broke over the left flank, smashed the Ree scouts back on the center, swept around the rear.

Reno flung up one blue arm. "Halt. Prepare to fight on foot. Dismount."

Now weary months of drill proved their worth. In mid-career the charge slithered to a dust-shrouded halt. Troopers swung out of their saddles, steady horseholders linked their mounts and trotted back. Carbines of the firing line blasted the surging assault. Blazing away, the battalion advanced a little, then recoiled. Those tremendous odds were not to be withstood. The blue fusillade slackened as cartridges jammed in overheated breaches, and grim troopers pried them out with knives. Oh, for even one of the Gatling guns now!

Backward ebbed the bending line, leaving blue heaps stranded on the prairie, back toward a strip of timber. There, perhaps, it could make a stand. Through the trees, troopers, glancing over their shoulders as they loaded, saw the river they had recently crossed. The water, glistening in the glare of the noonday sun, was an obstacle to further retreat, one to be passed only at deadly cost.

Copper bodies loomed through the smoke of battle—

screeching warriors rushing forward. Whistling arrows and bullets, buzzing like wasps, whipped and scourged the retreat. A trooper groaned, "Oh, God, I've got it!" and rolled over lifeless. Others tottered and dropped. Even the timber, now gained, furnished pitifully little shelter. The Indian scout, Bloody Knife, had just taken post by Reno's side when suddenly his brains were spattered over the officer.

It takes a staunch man to hold steady when another's brains are splashed over him. The swarthy major, unnerved, yelled an order to fall back. Only the nearest company heard him and mounted up. Other troopers on the firing line looked around and began to follow suit. Reno did not stay to organize a rearguard but, pistol in hand, galloped back to the river through red men thronging to close off the avenue of escape.

The retreat disintegrated into a disorderly rout. A lieutenant and a group of troopers were cut off and abandoned in the woods. Indian fire emptied saddle after saddle. The battle broke up into hand-to-hand, single combats, soldier against warrior. Red horsemen thrust in from all sides, grappled with galloping cavalrymen, dragged them from their mounts. One private, his horse killed by a howling Sioux, struggled to his feet and shot his adversary. As the brave fell, the trooper caught his pony, vaulted on to its back and won clear.

A few heroic men tried to stem the red torrent. The fine old scout, Charley Reynolds, faced it, rifle cracking, till it swept over him. Lieutenant McIntosh, commanding the rearmost company, kept rallying his troopers up to the moment that Sioux bullets riddled him. Dripping knives and tomahawks hacked his body to pieces because of his Indian blood. There galloped young Lieutenant Varnum through the turmoil, striving to head off the panicky flight, begging men to stand and save their comrades. Major Reno snapped at him, "I'm in command here," and led the rout on to the river.

No time to reach the ford, further downstream, now. Cavalrymen spurred wild-eyed horses over the brink of a five-foot bank into the river. On through it dashed the foremost and scrambled up the slopes of a hill beyond. On their heels, more men and horses plunged into the reddening waters. Lieutenant Hodgson's charger was hit and sank. He grabbed a trooper's stirrup and was pulled through, but as he gained the farther bank, an Indian bullet killed him.

On the hill beyond the river, the breathless, battered battalion made a stand at last, counting its losses. Three officers and twenty-nine troopers and scouts were dead, seven wounded, and fifteen missing. Its casualties were nearly fifty per cent.

II

Custer, at the head of his five companies, forged onward at a pounding gallop. Peter Shannon, riding to his left rear, could read the exhilaration of approaching battle, the promise of victory, in the very set of those buckskin shoulders. The cavalcade surged up a ridge and reined in to an abrupt halt.

Down in the valley before them, just beyond the river, lay the vast village. It was almost empty. Only squaws and children, catching sight of the cavalry on the bluffs, scurried about in alarm. The mass of the warriors had been drawn off to battle Reno when he charged toward the further end of the village. Here beckoned golden opportunity. Custer's luck!

The General's eagle eyes swept the horizon. Nowhere was either of the other two blue columns in view. One of Tom Custer's sergeants was called out of ranks and sent racing back to find Benteen, with orders to bring up the pack-train and its ammunition at once. Down-swung arms signaled forward. Bays, sorrels, and grays, still blowing, responded to gripping knees. Troopers' hands felt for the flap of revolver holsters. Only a little further, and a thundering charge could sweep through the Indian village like a spring freshet.

The old, familiar dryness parched Peter's throat, and his stomach muscles were taut. A gesture from Custer suddenly wrenched him from his abstraction, and he trotted forward. The General was speaking to Cooke.

"Sergeant Kanipe might miss Benteen. We'll play it safe. All right, Shannon, I'm sending you, too. Your mount's in good shape. Get back to Benteen and tell him to bring up that ammunition in a hurry. Ride hard!"

Peter, saluting, was whirling Justin when Cooke called, "Wait." Good adjutants put orders on paper—then there can be no mistake. Hastily Cooke scribbled:

"Benteen. Come on. Big village. Be quick. Bring packs. "P.S. Bring pac's."

The trumpeter snatched the message. A rapid flurry of hoofbeats and he was off, bent low over his mount's neck. Not until two days later would he realize that the paper he clutched was his own reprieve from death.

III

In the steady rhythm of Justin's gallop was comfort and reassurance, but anxiety tore at Peter's heart. He knew the general direction, yet Benteen had been in motion and his whereabouts was uncertain. The ridges and ravines of the valley of the Little Big Horn masked Peter's view like a blindfold. There was no time to ride up on a hill and look around. He could only trust the bearings he had been foresighted enough to take. He told himself: I can't fail. Patting

Justin's lathering neck, he plunged into a long ravine.

As he rode on, three Indians entered the further end of the ravine, blocking his path.

Immediately they whooped and rode swiftly toward him. It was too late to pull up, swing around and retreat. The warriors would sweep down on his back. Peter tugged his revolver out of its holster and dug unaccustomed spurs into Justin's flanks. The black Morgan spurted forward.

Disobeying the gestures of their leader, two of the braves galloped against Peter. The third pulled up to wait in the exit, making sure, ready for the cavalryman on the chance he might fight his way through his first assailants.

The onrushing pair drew apart to converge on their victim, right and left. One brandished a war club. The other, armed with a rifle, fired as he rode. As the bullet whistled past his cheek, Peter leveled his Colt, making himself hold his fire. At thirty yards he put three rounds into the rifleman, saw him fling up his arms and topple backwards with a shriek over his pony's rump.

But now the other warrior was upon him. Peter, reining Justin in, barely avoided a crushing impact from the charging pony. The black, stride broken, stumbled but recovered. The agile Indian pony kept his feet also, and his rider spun him around and charged again. Peter's revolver blazed thrice. He saw all three bullets thud into the painted chest, yet the Sioux still retained the strength to smash at him with his war club. It struck Peter's right shoulder a glancing blow, but its wielder, following its downward sweep, slid to the ground, dead.

Peter, his fingers numb, dropped his empty Colt. He saw the remaining warrior trotting slowly toward him and grasped the strap to unsling his carbine. Groaning, he found he could not raise his right arm. While he strove to reach the carbine with his left, his knees gathered Justin for a dash.

His chance of getting past was slim, but he must take it—he must get through to Benteen.

Then, suddenly he recognized the third warrior. Despite the warpaint on the stained skin, he could not doubt those features he knew so well. It was Rick.

Rick knew him in the same instant. His teeth bared in the old wolfish smile. He covered his enemy with his revolver but still did not shoot, relishing this long-awaited moment. Peter took advantage of the respite and spurred Justin off to the flank to pass him. But the other was ready for him there. He kicked the strong pinto he was riding straight across the path, so that Peter had to pull his horse back on his haunches. Quickly the trumpeter tried the other side, and again Rick neatly blocked him. Nothing could have delighted the renegade more than this cat-and-mouse game. He had his foe at his mercy, revolver gone, obviously unable to unsling his carbine.

As Peter circled back for another try, Rick raised his revolver. His eyes showed that he had enjoyed enough sport and was going to end it. Peter set himself to duck when he saw the trigger finger tightening, though he knew that a crack shot like Rick could scarcely miss. The gun banged, echoing against the walls of the ravine.

Unbelievably, Rick did miss. Anticipation of his triumph, the very fervor of his hatred, had spoiled his aim. Peter drove Justin forward in a last desperate dash.

Neither man had seen the shape that stood silhouetted against the sky for a moment on one wall of the ravine, nor did they still notice when it came swiftly slithering down. Its hide blending with the prairie soil, it stood regarding them, ears pricked forward. Then it ran toward them in great bounds.

How Bran had found his way to the valley from the distant Powder River base, no man could say. Other dogs have

Bran streaked in and launched himself upward in a mighty leap

made journeys as far and farther in search of their masters—guided by a mysterious canine instinct, driven by incomparable devotion. Now that Bran had come, he knew his duty. Yonder he had seen what appeared to be a painted Indian trying to kill his master. Long-enduring strength, bred into staghounds for centuries, revived in his weary sinews, as he flashed forward.

Peter had managed to skirt his enemy and was in the clear. Behind him he heard thundering hoofs. Rick, on his fresh horse, could not help but overtake him and would shoot him in the back. Perhaps when he was hit he could hang on somehow and get through to Benteen. He spoke to Justin, begging him for his utmost speed, and the black Morgan valiantly gave it.

Rick, galloping hard, waited for a sure shot—waited a little too long. Bran covered the last few yards in a terrific rush, streaked in and launched himself upward in a mighty leap. Like the staghound of *The Talisman,* hurtling at the throat of the traitorous Conrade, Marquis of Montserrat, Bran clamped his jaws on the neck of the renegade.

Looking back, Peter saw the deserter reeling under that ferocious attack, yet even as he fell, firing shot after shot into the tawny hide. His last glimpse as he rode out of the ravine showed him Rick prone on the prairie, his throat torn out, and beside him the still body of the gallant staghound.

Corporal-Trumpeter Shannon, 7th U.S. Cavalry, galloped on, tears streaming from his eyes. And in his head rang the words of Custer that day Bran had been brought to the hospital, and the General spoke for the dog.

"Soldier, he's saying, 'Master, you saved my life, and I'll guard yours with mine as long as we both shall live.'"

Captain Benteen and his column were advancing at a trot when Peter sighted them and galloped up to deliver his despatch. The officer read it as he rode.

"Right," he said. "Mighty glad you came. I got the first message, but I'm lost. Been trying to find the General everywhere. Confounded country's cut up so bad with gulleys, I can't get sight of him. Lead on, Corporal."

Benteen's shrewd glance scanned the soldier beside him. "You and your horse look like you've had hard going, Shannon. What happened?"

"Ran into three er—Indians in a ravine, sir. Had to ride through 'em. But we're all right." This was not the time to tell of the death of Rick and Bran.

"Was the General in action when you left?"

"Not yet, sir. He was just about to strike the village. It's a big one, but it was almost empty. He'll charge right through it and hit the Indians at the other end or wherever they are."

"Good." Benteen was about to command, "Gallop," when several of his Indian scouts dashed up, gesticulating. From the direction in which they pointed, a breeze faintly carried the sound of firing.

Benteen obeyed the maxim of Napoleon and marched to the sound of the guns. It led him not toward Custer but to the hill where Reno's routed troops were making their stand.

19: STRICKEN FIELD

CEASE FIRING

I

CUSTER, once he had despatched his second courier, Corporal-Trumpeter Shannon, paused a moment to scan with gleaming blue eyes the big Indian village across the river. What could balk him now? Surely, Benteen would gallop up with the pack-train before long. Even now Reno must be riding to attack the further end of the village. Exultant, the General gripped the sides of his favorite charger, Vic, and led his five companies toward the river, where a ford offered easy passage.

A few mounted Sioux bobbed up in front, wheeled their ponies and cut off at a tangent, riding for dear life. The General let them go. But from a ridge to his flank, rifle fire crackled.

Halt! Custer, with victory seemingly in his grasp, was cautious for once, suspecting an ambush. Dismounted skirmishers pushed up the slope to clear the way.

On the crest, four Cheyennes—four brave men alone—blazed away at the advancing cavalrymen. One trooper fell to their fire. For a little while the warriors held up the attack, then turned and fled. Short as the time was, it proved to be one of those fatal delays that alter the fortunes of battles. Racing messengers had reached and warned Chief Crazy Horse. Scarcely had Custer mounted his men again, when up the valley swept the tumultuous red horde, yelping in triumph from Reno's bloody repulse.

On they came, galloping madly, all the furious Sioux and Cheyennes. They poured in through the treacherous gullies, swooping down on Custer's flanks, menacing his front, shrieking war whoops, loosing a stream of lead and arrows.

Steady, the Seventh! In the face of those heavy odds, Custer ordered a retreat toward a hill. One company dismounted, then a second. Smoking carbines held off red charges, while the balance of the battalion climbed the slopes.

"Too many Indians"—Indians everywhere. They came cascading in through the ravines, enveloping the cavalrymen. Rifles of hidden savages spat down from the ridges. Troopers gasped and died. Wounded horses screamed in agony. Ammunition was dwindling fast. And still Benteen did not come.

Red charges wiped out the remnant of Keogh's company, then Calhoun's. Smith's gray horse company was rushed and smothered. Higher up the slopes, surviving troopers led their mounts into a semicircle to form a barricade and shot them. For a time they fired over the carcasses. They did not last long.

Wild, yipping warriors converged on Custer and the few beside him, making their last stand near the summit of the hill. On the lower slope, war clubs rose and struck, smashing in the skulls of prostrate figures in blue. Crazy Horse and Gall and Rain-in-the-Face waved their braves on for the final rush.

Perhaps—no white man lived to tell the tale—Custer at the end stood alone near the knoll. Certainly, tall and soldierly, utterly fearless as always, he fought to the last, his revolvers blazing, until bullets pierced his head and side and he fell.

It was all over in one brief, desperate hour. On the battle-field of the Little Big Horn, Custer lay slain and about him, like a feudal chieftain, were strewn the bodies of his kinsmen, his captains, and his men-at-arms.

II

Chance, haphazard as a flipped coin, had directed Benteen to Reno instead of to Custer. Through many years after the Battle of the Little Big Horn, men would speculate on that disastrous defeat and wonder what might have happened had Benteen joined Custer. In all likelihood, both battalions would have been wiped out by the onrush of the Indians upon that stricken field, carved by treacherous ravines.

Undoubtedly, Benteen's arrival saved Reno—that and the fact that Crazy Horse had drawn off the bulk of his warriors to attack Custer. Reno's casualties were heavy, his ammunition dangerously scarce. The troopers with Benteen quickly divided up their cartridges with their comrades, and soon a plentiful supply was assured, as the lagging pack-train trotted up. Peter was glad to catch sight of Old Pizen, grotesque in his harness, in the line of mules.

Feverishly, the two battalions began entrenching themselves on the hill, a good defensive position. Wounded men, the horses, and the mules were placed in a hollow, which offered a certain amount of protection from Indian bullets. From the timber across the river and other points surrounding the besieged, warriors, left by Crazy Horse to hold Reno in check while he dealt with Custer, kept up a wickedly harassing fire.

Benteen's bushy white brows lowered, as he watched his senior, Reno. The dark major, wrought up almost beyond control, was banging away with his revolver at Indians a thousand yards away. Before him, as the aftermath of his behavior on this bloody day, stretched bitter, sinister years. A court-martial would acquit him of charges of cowardice, based on his rout, but he would in later years be tried twice for conduct unbecoming an officer and a gentleman; and finally, drinking and brawling, he would be dismissed from the Army in disgrace, to die in poverty and misery.

At once, Captain Benteen took over command in all but name. It was he who became the bulwark of a defense soon to wax desperate.

Every officer, every trooper, was anxiously demanding: Where is Custer? The two couriers, Kanipe and Shannon, told where they had left him. And now, far up the valley, they heard heavy firing. Three crashing volleys punctuated it. That must be Custer in action.

Angry mutterings spread through the troops on the hill. "That's Custer." . . . "Let's get moving." . . . "Got to get to him."

Reno stood hesitant, undecisive. Captain Weir started off with his company, not waiting for orders. Reluctantly, prodded by Benteen, Reno gave command to follow. Since they could not leave the wounded, comrades laid the bandaged men on blankets, with six troopers grasping the edges of each. They moved out at a snail's pace.

Too slow, perforce, and too late. Before the column had advanced far, the mass of the Sioux and Cheyennes came galloping back in fierce, victorious frenzy from the annihilation of Custer and his men. Warriors by the hundred swooped down on the advancing Weir, smashed him back on the column. Only a gallant rear-guard action under Lieutenants Godfrey and Hare kept the retreat from becoming a second rout.

Back on the hill once more, cavalrymen of the Seventh fought for their lives. On through the day, a grim day that seemed to have no end, carbines spat from trenches around the slopes. An answering hail of Indian bullets poured in from the woods and higher ground. The war chiefs knew no lack of guns and ammunition now—Custer's dead had armed them. One after another, troopers slumped in their rifle pits, lay still or called feebly for first aid. Casualties rose alarmingly—eighteen killed, forty-three wounded.

Blessed dusk at last. In the hollow, the wounded moaned pitifully for water. Thirsty troopers on the firing line rolled pebbles in their mouths. Most canteens had long since run dry, and there was no place to refill them except the river yonder, and from its further bank Indian sharpshooters, concealed in the woods, maintained a rattling, pinging fire that seldom slackened.

Water they must have. The risk loomed large, but it must be taken, taken while there was still light enough for carbines on the hill to cover a dash to the river. Benteen called for volunteers from the group around him.

Peter said to himself: Somebody has to go. He stepped forward. At his side, he found Lieutenant Trelford and just behind him, Jim Galt, his old friend from first days at Fort Abe, and four others.

"Not you, Trelford," Benteen refused. "I can't spare an officer. Nor you, Galt—not with that game leg. Shannon, your shoulder limbered up? All right. You and the rest. Pick up all the canteens you can carry. Creep down that ravine.

At the end, run to the river for all you're worth. We'll cover you with everything we've got. Good luck."

Peter and the other volunteers, loaded with canteens, moved down through the ravine. Hearts pounded faster as they reached its outlet, and the deadly open space stretched before them.

"Come on!" Peter yelled and sprinted for the water.

Bullets kicked up dust around the runners. Over their heads whistled lead from the covering carbines of the Seventh. They threw themselves flat on the riverbank, submerged the canteens they clutched in the water. Bubbling and gurgling, the canteens took an eternity to fill. At last stoppers were pushed in. Carriers jumped to their feet and dashed for the ravine, dodging from side to side. Every blow on their spines of their jangling loads seemed the prelude to a smashing Indian bullet.

Panting, they staggered into the safety of the gulley and delivered their precious burdens. "Well done," came Benteen's praise. Peter and the other volunteers, breathing hard, knowing they were lucky to have made it unhit, returned to their places in the thin, extended firing line.

All that night the defenders of the hill fought on. Indians seldom attacked in the dark, but not a trooper of the Seventh dared to be caught off guard. The crimson spurts of encircling red rifles flashed around them. Yonder in the valley, leaping shapes were silhouetted by fires—warriors cavorting in triumphant scalp dances. Yet the night brought one cheering event. Lieutenant De Rudio and the troopers who had been cut off with him in the timber during the retreat and had lain hidden there stole out and managed to rejoin their comrades on the hill.

On through the black hours constantly recurred a sound, more nerve-wracking than the whistling bullets or the savage whooping of the scalp dancers—discordant blasts of a trumpet. At first, exhausted troopers raised heads in hope that the blaring heralded a rescue by relieving troops. Soon they realized that some Indian was sounding those calls to mock them.

Peter, listening in his rifle pit, felt his flesh creep. The dead body of one of his fellow-trumpeters must have been stripped of that instrument. But for Bran, it might have been his.

III

At first daylight, a storm of whirring arrows and bullets, pinging viciously, broke on the besieged with redoubled intensity. Brief squalls of rain beat down to tantalize the thirsty. Captain Benteen walked coolly around the circuit of entrenchments, ordering men to keep under cover as they fired. An Irish sergeant called to him:

"Captain, sor, ye tell us to kape down. It's yourself should do that. They'll git ye."

Benteen answered with a grin. "Oh pshaw, they can't hit me." He strode on unscathed, but a bullet ploughed through the sergeant's leg, smashing the bone.

Closer, steadily closer, crawled the Sioux and Cheyenne riflemen. On the north side of the hill, they slipped in near enough to launch a charge. The furious red onrush almost carried the trenches. One bold warrior came hurtling through the blue line and counted coup on a soldier he had killed before he himself was riddled.

Captain Benteen forced Reno to order a counterattack. It was the white-haired officer who led it personally. He stood up under heavy fire, while troopers crouched for a spring out of the trenches, and shouted above the din.

"All ready now, men. Now's your time. Give 'em hell. Hep, hep, here we go!"

They surged forward cheering—all but one trooper, who

lay in his rifle pit, crying like a child. Before that valiant sortie, the savages gave way and fled. Not one man in the assaulting wave was hit, and set faces relaxed into grins, as Benteen and his men came back on the double to the position. There they found the soldier, who had been unable to make himself join his charging comrades, inert in his rifle pit, an Indian bullet through his head.

It was only a respite, that charge. From bluffs above the hill, red snipers poured in fire from repeating rifles, bought from Rick and other white traders. Outranged carbines vainly replied. Indian bullets dropped more of the defenders, and horses and mules in the hollow reared, kicked and collapsed under the hail of death.

From between his jutting blinders, Old Pizen glared about him. He was thirsty and tired of standing under the weight of two cases of ammunition, packed on his back, so that cartridges could be rushed to one of the more distant parts of the firing line in an emergency. Now he smelled the slaughter around him, and decided it was high time he left this place. Cleverly he unloosed the knot of his tie-rope with his teeth and trotted out of the hollow and on through the position.

"Stop that mule!" an officer shouted. The loss of two cases of precious ammunition would be a catastrophe.

Old Pizen was not accustomed to being stopped by anybody when he had made up his mind. Troopers made futile grabs for his halter. The mule dodged others trying to head him off. He cleared a front-line barricade like a steeplechaser and with stubborn determination loped toward the Indian lines.

Out there in the open, he met swarms of those same leaden wasps which had tried to sting him in the hollow. Old Pizen emitted a defiant bray and went for them. His charge and his fearsome appearance in big, flapping blinders seemed to

"Stop that mule!" an officer shouted. The loss of two
cases of precious ammunition would be a catastrophe

have dismayed the wasps in front, for no more buzzed at him. Warriors held their fire and waited, grinning, for this strange creature to bring them two free cases of ammunition.

Hoofs thudded behind him. Pizen recognized the black horse and rider, as they cut in front of him. Peter Shannon had hastily bridled Justin, mounted him bareback and raced after the long-eared recreant.

But Pizen was not returning to that hill, not even for a friend. The mule darted off at an angle. Peter, in hot pursuit, headed him again. Old Pizen, like a full-rigged schooner, came about on the opposite tack.

Flights of wasps descended on them, buzzing more wickedly than ever. Peter heard faint shouts from the trenches, "Come in, come in!" He rode on in that crazy, reckless chase. The black Morgan, responding to rein and knee, was deft as a polo pony, but Old Pizen, laden though he was, matched him. Again and again, Peter missed his grasp for the dangling tie-rope. For an incredible twenty minutes, the chase continued. Once Pizen was blocked off so close to the Indian line that yelping redskins rose to drag Peter from his horse. He whirled and galloped clear of clutching hands.

On the next turn, Peter caught the rope at last. Old Pizen gave one final, indignant tug, then allowed himself to be led back up the slope, through cheering troopers and into the hollow. Peter, wondering why he was still alive, slid from Justin's back and, leaning on his horse, steadied himself while he weakly patted a heaving, black flank. Somebody came up behind him. Peter turned to look into Benteen's flushed face and to feel the firm clasp of the captain's hand, wringing his.

IV

The battle-weary men on the hill could scarcely believe their senses. That storm of arrows and bullets, which had beaten down on them for so many hours, was dying away into fitful gusts. Dashes to the river for water drew only desultory bursts of fire now.

Down in the valley they sighted billowing smoke—the Indians had fired the prairie grass. Through the dun pall, the Seventh beheld the host of the Sioux and Cheyennes marching away, a dark, moving mass of horsemen, three miles long and almost a mile wide. Haggard officers and troopers stared incredulously and distrustfully after the vanishing foe. A few hoarse voices set up a cheer.

Stand fast! the word was passed along the entrenchments. It's an Indian trick.

All the rest of the day, all that night, they stood to arms. It seemed well they did, for next morning a long cloud of dust spiraled up along the valley. Troopers in the rifle pits grasped their carbines again and waited grimly. Now, as before, there could be no thought of surrender. Better to die fighting than be massacred.

Blue uniforms shone through the dust haze. Terry and Gibbon had come at last. The relieving force, horse and foot, wound up the hill.

Even the joy of rescue was dimmed by the anxious query each force put to the other: "Where's Custer?" No man could answer.

A party rode out, making a cautious reconnaissance. Lieutenant Godfrey leveled his field glasses toward the knoll which would be known as Custer Hill. It was dotted with objects which appeared to be white boulders. Another look, and the officer almost dropped his glasses. Laconically he announced, "The Dead!"

As they moved forward, Captain Weir murmured, "Oh, how white they look! How white!" Sadly they surveyed the stripped bodies of Custer and the two hundred and eleven officers and men of the Seventh, the civilians and scouts, who had died with him. All had been scalped and mutilated, save only Custer. Even in death, the Indians had respected him. Gazing down with the rest at the fallen leader, Peter gave him a last salute.

On all that stricken field remained no living creature. Wait—yonder stood a horse, head drooping beside the corpse of his master, a horse so sorely wounded that the Indians had not bothered to drive him off with their herds. It was Comanche, Captain Keogh's bay charger. Gently they tended his wounds and led him slowly back to camp. If he lived, he would be taken along with Reno's wounded troopers and put aboard the *Far West*, waiting on the Yellowstone River.

As the melancholy task of burial commenced, Peter strode up to Captain Benteen.

"Sir, Corporal Shannon requests permission to find and bury his dog."

Peter, after the battle ended, had told his commander about Bran's sacrifice in the ravine. Benteen's eyes softened. "Go ahead, Shannon," he granted permission.

Sorrowfully, Peter mounted Justin and retraced the ride he had made with Custer's last message. In the ravine, the two warriors he had shot still lay where they had dropped. The Indians, who had carried off all their other dead and wounded, had not discovered these two, nor the corpse of Rick. Beside the renegade, with his ghastly, torn throat, Peter saw the tawny form of his staghound.

The trumpeter dismounted and, with one hand resting on his saddle pommel, stood looking down at the hound's still body. Justin lowered his head in sympathy and sniffed at his canine friend. Tears welled up in Peter's eyes. It was supposed to be unmanly to cry, but no one was here to see. And if you loved a dog, a dog that had given his life for you, you had every right to mourn him from the depths of your heart. Peter bent down to stroke the shaggy form for the last time.

He gave a sudden start. Bran's body was still warm.

Peter grasped his canteen, raised the dog's head and poured water down his throat. In a little while, eyes, half glazed, opened and gazed into his. The feathered tail stirred in one feeble wag.

Quickly the trooper unrolled his blanket and folded it over Justin's withers in front of the saddle. As tenderly as he could, he lifted the limp staghound on to the padded rest. The strong Morgan, carrying double, walked with careful tread to the camp.

v

In a corner of the hold of the *Far West,* lay the charger, Comanche, and near him Bran reposed. Surgeons had treated them, and the spark of life, so near to extinction in both animals, had kindled again. Peter knew now that horse and dog would live to stand many a parade with the Seventh as honored veterans.

The trumpeter, going up on deck, gratefully reflected on Benteen's kindness in letting him, unwounded though he was, travel on the steamer to take care of his dog, while the unhurt survivors of the Seventh marched back to the post. He stood beside the pilot house where Captain Grant Marsh was conning the *Far West,* her paddle-wheels churning, through the muddy waters of the river. Someone came up and spoke his name. It was Lieutenant Trelford, heavily-bandaged right arm in a sling. Peter had heard how the officer got that wound, leading one of the charges that beat back the surge of the Sioux up Reno Hill.

"Shannon, Captain Benteen ordered me to give you these." Trelford pressed sergeant's chevrons into Peter's hand. "You deserve them—and a lot more."

"Thank you, sir."

"You're a good soldier, and I'll be the first to say so when the battle report goes in. Maybe that'll go part way toward evening us up for that time you shoved me clear of Old Pizen's heels."

The tall, handsome officer paused a moment, then went on more slowly. "Whether it squares us or not, I'm going to do something I've long intended doing when we get back to the fort. I'm telling you this as man to man—not as officer to trooper. We're both in love with the same girl. First chance I get, I'm going to ask her to marry me."

"It's decent of you to tell me, Lieutenant."

"Struck me as only fair. Good luck to you, Shannon— every place else."

Peter, turning, glanced from the chevrons in his hand to Trelford's shoulder straps. He walked away, thinking sober thoughts.

Sally Ann, an officer's daughter, a sergeant's wife, living on Soapsuds Row? No, he could not imagine it, nor would he ask it. He could not beg her to wait on the distant chance that he might win a commission some day. His attitude was not snobbery. He knew fine women on the Row—Ma Simmons, laundress and cook for the Lindsays, and Sergeant Pinchon's wife in the Fourth, others in the Seventh. Neither he nor Sally Ann were snobs. Yet it was inescapably true that you were happiest among people with interests in common with yours, people whose upbringing and education compared to such as you had been fortunate enough to have received.

Peter sighed deeply. Best buy out of the Service and go back to college. Maybe Sally Ann would marry him when he graduated and give up the Army life she loved.

20: STARRY RIBBON

TO THE COLOR OR STANDARD

I

CRISP autumn days had come again to Fort Abraham Lincoln. In the summer following the Battle of Little Big Horn, the Seventh, its ranks filled, had fought the Sioux again. In a forthcoming campaign, it would strike them once more, recapturing its lost guidons, redeeming defeat, restoring the proud tradition it would maintain on other battlefields in years ahead.

Peter Shannon stood in a doorway, gazing across the drill ground, his mind dwelling on the crowded events of the months that had passed since he returned to the post.

There was that stirring day he and others had been called out in front of the paraded regiment. General Terry had pinned a medal on his blouse, a medal whose blue ribbon gleamed with white stars, the Medal of Honor. The words of the citation rang again in his head like a paean. "Service performed in action, of such conspicuous character as to clearly distinguish the man for gallantry and intrepidity above his comrades . . . service that involved extreme jeopardy of life or the performance of extraordinarily hazardous duty." Words that signalized those minutes on Reno Hill—his gallop on Justin through the leaden wasps—perverse Old Pizen, caught at last.

Peter twisted his head to glance down at his shoulders. What he saw there brought back the later day, no less thrilling, when he opened a War Department envelope and scanned the lines on the crinkling paper within. "The President tenders Sergeant Peter Shannon, 7th U.S. Cavalry, a commission as Second Lieutenant in the United States Army . . ."

That had given him these gold-bordered shoulder straps he wore so proudly. And they, in turn, had carried him through to the happiness before him on this bright autumn day.

Peter's revery was interrupted by a figure in civilian clothes coming up behind him in the doorway. John Shannon said, "Time we reported for duty at the chapel, Lieutenant Shannon. Come on, my boy."

Father and son strode across the drill ground, walking in step like the soldiers they were.

The music of a prelude, pouring from a foot-pumped organ, filled the little chapel. Peter and John Shannon, bridegroom and best man, took their stand in the chancel. Peter glanced, smiling, at Mrs. Lindsay, at all the women of the post, and his comrades of the Seventh in the pews. There sat Phil Trelford, too, good loser and good sport. A wave of sadness swept Peter as he thought of those who were not present. His own dear mother—if only she had lived to see this day. The dashing, yellow-haired General, his commander and in many ways his idol. Mrs. Custer, forlorn but brave in her grief. Peter told himself that the first leave he got, he and Sally Ann would go to Michigan to see her and the faithful Eliza. A pity Eiza was missing this wedding she had looked forward to so eagerly. Peter's spirits rose as he imagined how Eliza would surely have broken in on the ceremony with a regular camp-meeting shout of "A-men! Praise the Lawd!"

The solemn and joyous strains of the wedding march resounded. Up the aisle on the arm of her father came Sally Ann. Peter knew that never had he beheld anyone so utterly lovely. The gleaming white satin of her wedding gown, with its piquant puffed sleeves, set off her trim little form. Her filmy veil flowed back, revealing her chestnut curls. Sally Ann's lips were parted in a faint, breathless smile, and her hazel eyes sought his, eyes that were shining with the promises she would give.

"For better for worse, for richer for poorer, in sickness and in health, to love and to cherish, till death us do part, according to God's holy ordinance; and thereto I plight thee my troth."

They took them, those tremendous vows, with all their young hearts, knowing that none had need to keep them more steadfastly than an Army girl and soldier on the frontier in the Indian wars.

The chaplain said the final words and stepped back. Peter bent and kissed his bride. They walked down the aisle, Sally Ann hugging her husband's arm tight. The last notes of the organ were drowned by the blare of the Seventh's band outside, striking up *Garryowen.* On through the door of the chapel they moved and underneath flashing steel where drawn sabres formed an arch. At its end waited the beaming Mac-Tavish, one hand grasping the bridle of a black horse, the other the leash of a tawny staghound.

AUTHOR'S AFTERWORD

Among the chief sources for this story's incidents and background were Mrs. Custer's books and my own *Indian-Fighting Army*. I have followed history quite closely except for some compression of time and the use of certain episodes, such as the mule race and the buffalo hunt, out of their chronological occurrence.

There is historical basis for the introduction of a dog on the battleground of the Little Big Horn. One chronicler quotes Burkman, Custer's orderly, as stating that when the staghounds were left at the 7th Cavalry's Powder River base, a yellow dog broke loose and trotted after the troops. A second historian adds that a dog, not an Indian one, was seen on the battlefield, moving among the dead.

The depiction of Custer and his actions in the campaign, over which controversy still rages, follows the presentation I made in *Indian-Fighting Army*.

I robbed Burkman of one of his functions, the care of Custer's dogs, to give it to my character, MacTavish. Special acknowledgment must be made of two other substitutions. In this story, my Peter Shannon replaces in the course of the battle two actual troopers of the Seventh, who must here be given credit for gallant deeds. It was Trumpeter John Martin (born Martini), who carried Custer's last message to Benteen. Sergeant Richard P. Hanley, Company "C," won the Medal of Honor for rounding up the fugitive ammunition mule under heavy fire on Reno Hill.

Brevet rank, now disused, was confusing in those days when it was conferred in lieu of a decoration for gallantry and it would be equally so in these pages. Consequently, except in the case of General Custer, whose actual rank in 1876 was lieutenant colonel, my narrative refers to officers of the

nth by their roster rank and employs their brevet desig-
tion only in direct discourse.

To this, my nineteenth book, my wife, Mildred Adams
Downey, gave the same invaluable help in criticism and typ-
ing as she has its predecessors. Again I am fortunate in having Paul Brown as illustrator. I am grateful for careful
editing to Dorothy Bryan, Dodd, Mead & Co., and for
checking by Sylvester Vigilante, American History Room,
New York Public Library, and by Oliver P. Swan, of Paul
R. Reynolds & Son; also for courtesies given by *Blue Book*
where a shortened version of this novel appeared.

FAIRFAX DOWNEY
New York City, 1948